Jessi and the Awful Secret

DISCARD

Jessi and the Awful Secret
Ann M. Martin

AN
APPLE
PAPERBACK

SCHOLASTIC INC.
New York Toronto London Auckland Sydney

Cover art by Hodges Soileau

ISBN 0-590-45663-6

12 11 10 9 8 7 6 5 4 3 2 1   3 4 5 6 7 8/9

Printed in the U.S.A.   40

First Scholastic printing, February 1993

The author gratefully acknowledges
Suzanne Weyn
for her help in
preparing this manuscript.

The author would like to thank
Dr. Adele M. Brodkin
for her sensitive evaluation of this book.

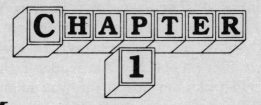

CHAPTER 1

Mme Noelle looked at me and rapped her stick sharply on the studio floor. She didn't have to say a word. Instantly I raised my leg even higher behind me and pushed my shoulders back. "Much better, Mademoiselle Romsey," she said with a nod. Then she moved along, studying the *grand battements* of the other students at the *barre*.

"You are much too stiff," I heard her tell a blonde girl named Mary Bramstedt. "Relax your shoulders. Breathe!"

Maybe I should explain a few things before I go any further. For starters, my name is not Mademoiselle Romsey. That's just how it comes out when my teacher, Mme Noelle, speaks to me in her French accent.

I'm Jessica Ramsey. All my friends call me Jessi. I'm eleven and (among other things) I take ballet lessons at a school in Stamford.

Mme Noelle is rather old and very strict, but

has a great reputation as a ballet teacher. In fact, the ballet school I go to is considered one of the best on the East Coast. (Not counting the professional schools down in New York City.) I'm really glad to be studying here.

Right now I attend class every Tuesday and Friday, after school. My dad works in Stamford and picks me up on the way home. It takes us about a half hour to drive from Stamford to our home in Stoneybrook.

Mme Noelle clapped her hands and I swung my leg out of the *grand battement* position. A *grand battement* is a warm-up exercise meant to loosen the hips and hamstring muscles of the legs. (It's pronounced, "grand-bot-a-mont," which is French, the language of ballet.)

Class always opens with a series of warm-ups. It's important that a dancer's muscles be warm and stretched so she doesn't hurt herself (or himself — though there are only girls in my class) during the more difficult work that comes later.

"Before we begin ze center work," Mme Noelle said that day, "I have an announcement to make. Ze Stamford Ballet School will be giving a free six-week donce class to some of Stamford's less privileged children. Ze class will be held every Tuesday at zis time. We need volunteers to help Mme Dupre conduct it."

2

"What about our own work?" Katie Beth Parsons asked.

"Volunteers will receive six free classes to make up for ze ones zey will miss," Mme Noelle explained.

"But won't we fall behind?" asked Carrie Steinfeld.

"You must make zis decision for yourself," Mme Noelle told her. "At some point in your careers, many of you will wish to teach. Zis will be a valuable experience. Now, do I have any volunteers?"

Immediately my hand shot up. I love working with kids. I baby-sit a lot and I even belong to a group called the Baby-sitters Club. (The club is really important to me. Maybe not as important as ballet, but close. I'll tell you about it later.)

I wasn't worried about falling behind in my work. As it is, I'm the youngest in the class. (Katie Beth used to be, before I joined the class, but she's a year older than me. I think she resents not being the youngest anymore.) And — though I wouldn't say this to anyone else — I'm one of the best. I don't mean to sound conceited. It's just true. Not long ago I danced the lead in *Sleeping Beauty* in the school production. I've had other lead parts as well.

The only other girl who raised her hand was Mary Bramstedt.

To be honest, I was pretty surprised by two things. The first was that more girls didn't volunteer. Teaching kids to dance sounded like so much fun, I couldn't believe everyone wouldn't want to do it. I guess they didn't want to take time away from their own classes. (I know dancers have to be serious and competitive, but sometimes I think they take that too far.)

The second thing that surprised me was that Mary *did* volunteer. She's nice enough, but very intense. She's a perfectionist who worries about getting every step exactly right. And the odd thing is, she's not one of the best dancers in class. Not by far. For all her worrying, she's stiff and sort of robotlike when she dances. It's as if she can't stop worrying long enough to let the music carry her. I wouldn't have expected Mary to feel comfortable taking even a moment away from her regular classes. But — as I said — she surprised me, which made me like her a little better than I had.

"Very good," Mme Noelle said to Mary and me. "Report here next Tuesday and Madame Dupre will meet you."

Then she nodded toward our new piano player in the corner of the room, a thin young man with glasses. He began to play as we took our places in the center of the studio.

4

We spaced ourselves evenly and began work on a ballet move called an *arabesque penché*. We raised one leg way up behind us while we leaned forward for balance. Of course, our arms had to be carefully placed so we didn't topple over.

Mary was in front of me and I noticed her supporting leg was quivering badly. I wanted to suggest she shift her weight backward a bit, but Mme Noelle frowns on any talking during class.

From there we worked on *pirouettes* (which are turns, pronounced "peer-oh-ets") and jumps. Finally we came to my favorite part of class. At the end of class each of us dances alone across the studio doing a series of steps that Mme Noelle has strung together. Today her instruction was: *Bourée* with *port de bras*, into a *pas de chat*, ending with *arabesque penché* in first *arabesque* position.

It sounds complicated, doesn't it? But it really isn't, not once you know what the terms mean. Mme Noelle wanted us to take tiny steps on our toes while moving our arms gracefully up and down. That's the *bourée* with *port de bras*.

Pas de chat means "step of the cat." It's really fun to do. You jump in the air, touch your toes together lightly, then come down softly.

5

After the *pas de chat*, Madame simply wanted us to go into the *arabesque* position we'd practiced during class.

I stood in line, and when my turn came I danced out into the middle of the room. When I'm not just doing moves, but actually dancing, it's as if my body does all the thinking. My mind shuts off and just hears the music. All the things I've learned about dance seem to be stored in my arms and legs, not in my brain. "You make that look so easy," said Lisa Jones after I finished my steps.

"Thanks," I replied. Lisa had gone before me. She'd done pretty well except that she stumbled backward a little when she came down from her *pas de chat*.

Lisa is one of the nicest girls in class, but the truth is, I'm not very close to her or any of the others. I've always felt like a bit of an outsider.

Since I'm the youngest and newest member of the class, I suppose it's natural that I would feel like an outsider. And then, being black sets me apart from the other girls, too. Not that anyone has ever even mentioned it to me, but all you have to do is look in the practice mirror to see it. One cocoa-colored face with dark eyes standing among the other white faces.

I was never so aware of the color of my skin

6

until we moved to Stoneybrook. Our old neighborhood back in New Jersey was very integrated. Being black just wasn't an issue. But it became a big issue once my family moved to Stoneybrook.

We came because my dad's company transferred him to Stamford. (The transfer included a big promotion, so he was happy about it.) My sister Becca (she's eight) and I weren't nearly as excited. (My brother Squirt is just a baby, so he didn't care one way or the other.)

Besides leaving our family and friends (like my cousin Keisha who was both family and my best friend), we had to adjust to a new school and a new neighborhood. Believe me, some people in Stoneybrook weren't one bit glad to see a black family move into their all-white neighborhood. It was rough at first. But we stuck it out and now everything is mostly okay.

But, getting back to the girls in my class, I never quite felt I belonged in their group. I tried not to mind. After all, I had my friends at school and in the BSC. (That's what we call the Baby-sitters Club.) I even have a great best friend, Mallory Pike. I told myself I didn't need any more friends, but the truth was I sometimes felt a little lonely at my ballet school.

When class ended, we applauded Mme Noelle and then went to the dressing room.

"That was nice of you to volunteer," Carrie Steinfeld said to me as we walked down the hall. "I would have but I can't afford the time away from lessons."

Carrie is the oldest girl in class. I know she's nervous these days. She's about to graduate but she's never had a leading role in a production. Because of that it's going to be hard for her to get into a school for older students or to be invited to a professional dance company. It's a shame, because she's a good dancer. But in ballet, being good isn't always enough. You have to be great.

I didn't want Carrie to feel bad, so I made light of volunteering. "It's a good excuse to goof off a little," I joked. "And it sounded like fun."

"No way," Katie Beth disagreed, wrinkling her nose. "You wouldn't catch me teaching a bunch of screaming brats."

"I'm sure they're not all brats," said Mary. "I think it's generous of the school to offer the program. Helping out is the least I can do."

I suddenly had the feeling I was going to like working with her.

In the dressing room everyone changed quickly. It's interesting to see how ten girls can go from looking all alike, with black leotards, pink tights, toe shoes, and hair pulled back off our faces, to looking very, very different once we're dressed. Katie Beth, for example wears tight leggings and big bold tops, while Lisa dresses in nothing but jeans and sweaters.

"I just can't get high enough on the *pas de chat*," I heard Mary complain as she sat on the bench and pulled off her toe shoes. She was talking to a tall, thin girl named Mindy Howard.

"I know what you mean," Mindy said, pulling on her long-sleeved T-shirt. "I had the same problem until I lost ten pounds. Then I was fine."

Mary got up and examined herself in the full-length mirror. "I probably could drop some of this fat around my middle," she observed.

What fat? I thought. I couldn't see a smidge of fat anywhere on her. She didn't have *two* pounds to lose — forget about losing ten!

"Losing the weight makes a big difference," Mindy told Mary. "You'll see."

Personally, I didn't think Mindy jumped all that high even now. Which meant her weight loss theory didn't hold up. And losing weight wasn't the solution to Mary's problem, either. If she wanted to jump higher, she should simply practice jumping higher. That's what I would have told her. But she hadn't asked me, and I felt I would have been rude to butt into their conversation.

Mary turned her back to the mirror and then craned her neck around to see herself. "I have a fat rear end, too," she muttered.

She did not!

"All that weighs you down," Mindy said as if she were an authority on the subject.

I couldn't believe what I was hearing.

Really, it's not that unusual, though. There's a *look* in ballet — dancers are thin, square-shouldered, and have a more-or-less oval face. I've heard that it started because the great choreographer George Ballanchine wanted his *corps de ballet* (all the dancers who aren't the stars) to look alike. Since his death, this has started to change. That's what people say, anyway. It seems to be true.

A lot of girls go crazy worrying about what they'll look like once their bodies finish changing and developing. They might not wind up with the right kinds of bodies for ballet. That's rough when you consider that most dancers have been studying since they were four or so. All of a sudden they have to rethink their plans.

I don't worry about it too much. Luckily I seem to be naturally thin and so is everyone in my family. (Except Aunt Cecelia who lives with us and helps take care of Becca and Squirt while Mama works. Keep your fingers crossed that I don't take after her.)

Of course, it's easy for me to not worry. I have a couple of years yet before my body will start seriously changing. Still, when the time comes, I sure hope I won't be as crazed about it as Mindy and Mary.

CHAPTER 2

Fridays are always a challenge for me. I dart out of ballet class and hope my dad is right on time to pick me up. (He usually is.) Then I have to work very hard not to fidget if we're not going fast enough. The reason I'm in such a rush is that I have to be at my BSC meeting by five-thirty. Sharp!

Kristy Thomas, our club president, is very big on punctuality. She gives you a Look if you're late. Those looks are so withering that I'd do just about anything to avoid getting one. Unfortunately, I've experienced the Look on several Fridays when I scooted in a couple of minutes late. Sometimes there's no way out of rush-hour traffic in downtown Stamford. But try telling that to Kristy.

That Friday I arrived at five-thirty on the dot. Whew! I practically flew into the room, and took my usual spot on the floor of Claudia Kishi's bedroom — our BSC meeting place.

"You made it in the nick of time once again," whispered my friend Mallory, who is also a BSC member. She knows how harried Fridays are for me.

I smiled as I put my hand over my pounding heart. "The green lights were with us," I replied, panting. "One yellow light and it would have been all over." (My dad always stops at the yellow lights instead of zooming through them the way I'd like him to. It drives me crazy when I'm in a hurry.)

"The meeting will now begin," Kristy said from Claudia's director's chair. She always sits in that chair with a pencil stuck over her ear and a visor on her head.

Claudia, Mary Anne, and Dawn were seated on Claudia's bed. Stacey was propped on the edge of Claudia's desk, by the phone. Before I go any further, I should probably tell you a little about my BSC friends. After that, I'll explain how the club itself works.

Since Mal is my best friend, I'll start with her. She has curly, reddish-brown hair, freckles, and wears braces (the clear kind), and glasses. (She's dying for contacts but so far her parents say she's too young.) Mallory doesn't consider herself pretty. She hates her nose in particular. But I think someday she'll be prettier than anyone imagines, and there's so much goodness *inside* Mallory that after you know her awhile, she starts to look pretty.

Mallory comes from a huge family. She's the oldest of eight kids! There are the triplets, Byron, Adam, and Jordan, who are ten. Even though they're identical it's easy to tell them apart once you get to know them. And it helps that they don't dress alike. Next comes Vanessa. She's nine and shares a room with Mal. After Vanessa is Nicky who's eight, Margo who's seven, and Claire who is five.

Mallory complains that there is nothing but "utter pandemonium," at her house, but I like visiting there. It's always lively and fun. I'm not sure I'd want to live at the Pike house, though. Mal doesn't get much privacy and that's hard on her.

Aside from all the usual reasons a person wants privacy, Mal has an extra need for it since she wants to be a writer. I should say she *is* a writer. One of her stories won the prize for "Best Overall Fiction" in the sixth grade during a Young Author's Day contest. Mallory dreams of someday writing and illustrating her own children's books. She's so creative that I'm sure she'll be great at it.

Mallory and I have a lot in common. We're both in the sixth grade at Stoneybrook Middle School. We both love to read, especially stories about horses. We also like mysteries, but hate horror stories. You couldn't ask for a better friend than Mallory.

The next person I'll tell you about is Kristy. As I said, she's the club president. She's president because the club was originally her idea and also because Kristy is naturally a presidential type person. She's always coming up with great ideas. She knows how to make them happen, too. Kristy is a doer not just a talker — although Kristy does talk a lot. You might even say she has a big mouth.

It might sound as if Kristy is a pain, but she's not. She has a great sense of humor and is really down-to-earth. And her "bossiness" is what keeps the club running so well.

For someone with such a big personality, Kristy is very petite. Although she's thirteen (just like all the other members besides Mal and me) she looks younger. She has longish brown hair and brown eyes. Her idea of fashion is jeans, sneakers, and a T-shirt or a sweater. She also wears either her visor or a baseball cap with a collie on it. You could call Kristy a tomboy. She loves sports and even coaches her own softball team for little kids called Kristy's Krushers. Boys aren't high on her list of interests — except she does like Bart Taylor who coaches a rival softball team.

From everything I've told you about Kristy,

here's something I bet you'd never guess. Kristy is rich. Her stepfather Watson Brewer is a millionaire!

Kristy didn't start off rich. In fact, Mr. Thomas, her father, up and left the family right after her little brother, David Michael, was born. Mrs. Thomas had to raise (and support) Kristy, her two older brothers, and David Michael all on her own. But Mrs. Thomas is like Kristy — a practical person with lots of energy. She got a good job in Stamford (one of those business kinds of jobs I don't always understand). And that's where she met Watson Brewer.

When Kristy was in the seventh grade, Mrs. Thomas married Watson. After that, the Thomases moved into Watson's mansion across town. At first Kristy wasn't thrilled about this — not Watson, not the move, not even the mansion. But now she likes Watson better and she's gotten used to her new home. She's also crazy about her new little stepbrother and stepsister, Andrew (who is four) and Karen (who is seven). They're Watson's kids from his first marriage. Most of the time, they live with their mother, but they spend every other weekend, holidays, and some vacation time with their father.

Kristy's family has just kept growing! Her mom and Watson adopted a little Vietnamese girl they named Emily Michelle. She's two and a half and totally adorable. Then Kristy's grandmother, Nannie, moved in to help take care of Emily Michelle while Watson and Kristy's mom are at work. And if you add in David Michael's puppy, Watson's cat, and the goldfish Karen and Andrew keep at the house, you've got a pretty huge family.

Talking about Kristy leads me right into telling you about Mary Anne Spier. That's because Kristy and Mary Anne have been best friends ever since they were little. They even look sort of alike. Mary Anne is also on the small side with brown hair and brown eyes. And Mary Anne used to have long hair like Kristy's, but she got it cut short recently.

Even though Mary Anne and Kristy are best friends, their personalities are quite different. Mary Anne isn't a big talker, but she's a great listener. She really cares about people and is very sensitive. (Mary Anne cries easily, especially when sad things happen to other people.)

Like Kristy, Mary Anne is now part of a blended family. Originally she was an only child. Her mother died when she was a baby and for most of her life her family consisted of her and her father. This wasn't always easy on Mary Anne since her father was pretty strict. But then something happened that changed Mary Anne's life. Dawn Schafer moved to town. She became Mary Anne's other best friend *and* her stepsister!

Here's how that happened. Dawn came to Stoneybrook from California when her parents got divorced. Mrs. Schafer had grown up in Stoneybrook and I guess she wanted to be nearer to her own parents after the divorce.

Dawn and her younger brother, Jeff, didn't like Stoneybrook at first. (I can understand how they felt. Moving isn't easy.) Their father was still in California along with everyone else they knew. And even now Dawn isn't completely comfortable with the cold weather. In fact, Jeff never did adjust to the changes. He returned to California to live with his dad.

Anyway, Mary Anne and Dawn soon became friendly. Mary Anne introduced Dawn to the other members of the club and she joined it, too. Then one day Mary Anne and Dawn were looking through Mrs. Schafer's old high school yearbook and they discovered an amazing fact. Dawn's mother and Mary Anne's father had dated in high school. More than dated. They'd been in love. It turned out that Mrs. Shafer's parents had sent her to college in California just to get her away from Mr. Spier. They thought he would never amount to anything. (They were sure wrong about that. Mr. Spier is a lawyer now.)

Mary Anne and Dawn decided to try to reunite their parents. This took some doing, but their plan worked. After dating for an eternity, the two of them got married. That's how Mary Anne and Dawn became stepsisters.

The Spiers moved into the Shafers' old farmhouse. (It was built in 1795 and has a secret passageway which leads from Dawn's room underground to the barn out back!) At first, Dawn and Mary Anne were thrilled. But then they discovered that blending two families isn't always easy. Dawn's mom didn't particularly like Mary Anne's cat, Tigger. There was also the mealtime issue. Dawn and her mom are health food nuts and only eat stuff like salads, tofu, and veggie burgers. (They think bacon is the grossest thing on earth.) Mary Anne and her dad eat regular food. So, just planning dinner became a big problem for their new family. Now all that is behind them and they're happy. Most of the time both Dawn and Mary Anne seem very pleased to be sisters. (By the way, just so you know — Dawn has long, long, white-blonde hair and a casually trendy way of dressing. She's totally gorgeous but isn't concerned about her looks at all. I like that about her.)

The next person I need to tell you about is Claudia Kishi. I find her totally fascinating. She's unlike anyone I've ever met.

First of all, Claud looks very distinctive. She's Japanese-American with beautiful, delicate features and long, silky straight black hair. That alone would be enough to make her striking. But Claudia adds to her natural beauty with her own artistic way of dressing. She puts colors and styles together in a unique way. (I'm not sure many people would look good dressing the way she does. On Claud, though, the look is very cool.) For example, today she was wearing a neon green tank top under a white oversized man's shirt and fuschia pink stirrup pants. The shirt was rolled at the sleeves and belted with a colorful woven belt.

Claud finished the outfit with dangly ceramic-bead earrings she'd made herself in pottery class. She's super artistic. She paints, sketches, draws, sculpts. You name it!

Besides art and cool clothing, Claudia loves junk food. Her parents disapprove of Ho-Ho's and Twinkies and stuff like that, so she hides them all over her room. You never know when you're going to pick up a pillow and find a bag of potato chips or something behind it. The other thing she stashes away are her Nancy Drew books. Her parents don't approve of those, either. They don't think the mysteries are "intellectual" enough.

Claudia couldn't care less if the books are "intellectual." One thing Claud is *not* interested in is school work. Although she can't spell for anything, she's definitely not dumb. She just doesn't like school. And, unfortunately, her grades show it. She's the complete opposite of her older sister, Janine, who is a genius. Janine has some sort of super I.Q. which is tough on Claudia.

Speaking of cool, Stacey McGill is right up there with Claudia. In some ways, she may be even cooler, since she's originally from New York City. Stacey and Claudia are best friends and they seem more sophisticated than the rest of us. Stacey wears her blonde hair in a perm. She has very trendy clothes, although they're not quite as artistic as Claudia's.

Like my family, Stacey's family came to Stoneybrook because her father's job was transferred to Stamford. She met Claudia and became part of the club. From then on, she started liking Stoneybrook, even though she still missed New York. Just when she really felt as if she belonged, her dad's company transferred him *back* to New York. So, Stacey said good-bye to everyone and moved back again. (Here's a coincidence — my family moved into her old house then!)

In New York, things didn't go too well for the McGills. I'm not sure why, but Stacey's parents decided to divorce. Mrs. McGill came back to Stoneybrook and Stacey came with her. Everyone in the BSC was happy to see her, of course.

Stacey has another problem. She's diabetic. She has to watch what she eats — no sweets at all. And, she has to give herself injections of insulin every day. I think that would really get me down, but most of the time Stacey is a very up-beat person.

Here's how our club works. We meet every Monday, Wednesday, and Friday from five-thirty to six in Claudia's room. Claudia is the only one of us who has a phone with a private number in her bedroom. That's why we meet here. It's also why Claudia is the vice-president.

During club hours, our clients call and set up baby-sitting appointments. It works out great for them because they can call just one number and reach seven baby-sitters instead of having to make a bunch of phone calls.

Actually, they're reaching nine sitters. We have two associate members of our club. They don't come to meetings but we call them if no one else is free to baby-sit. One of them is Logan Bruno. He's Mary Anne's boyfriend. (She's the only one of us who has a steady boyfriend.) The other associate is a girl named Shannon Kilbourne. She lives near Kristy and goes to a different school.

Mallory and I are junior officers. Because of

our age, we only sit during the day, which means after school or on weekends. This frees the others to take night jobs. (I can't wait until I'm old enough for night jobs. I won't feel like such a kid.)

So, anyway, our clients call and say when and what time they need a sitter. Then whoever answers the phone says she'll check it out and call right back. That's where Mary Anne comes in. She's the club secretary and keeps the record book in order. The book (another of Kristy's great presidential ideas) contains everyone's schedules—my ballet classes, Mallory's archery club meetings, Claudia's art classes, Kristy's softball games. If one of us has a dentist appointment or a big class project due, it goes into the book. Mary Anne then looks at the book and tells us who is free to take a particular baby-sitting job. She's very proud of the fact that she's never, ever, made a scheduling error.

The record book also lists the names and phone numbers of all our clients and any important information about the kids we sit for, like food allergies, fears, bedtimes, and stuff like that. It's a good thing to check before going on a job.

The only part of the book Mary Anne isn't responsible for is the record of money we've earned and spent. That's Stacey's department since she's the club treasurer (and our resident math whiz). Even though each of us takes home the money we earn, Stacey keeps track of it, just for the record. She also collects dues and puts the money in a big envelope.

No one likes to part with money but the dues are necessary. We use the money to pay Claudia's phone bill, and to pay Charlie Thomas (one of Kristy's older brothers) to drive Kristy to and from meetings now that she's moved out of the neighborhood. We also need to restock our Kid-Kits from time to time.

Kid-Kits are another of Kristy's brilliant ideas. We each have a box filled with coloring books, crayons, toys, and any little thing we think would amuse kids. Kristy noticed that kids like playing with other people's toys more than their own. That's how she came up with the idea and it really works. My Kid-Kit has saved more than one rainy day. Kid-Kits are also great for distracting fighting kids and cheering up tearful ones who don't want to part with their parents.

As I said, Kristy is president because she never stops thinking up these great ideas.

Dawn is our alternate officer. She steps in if any of the other officers is absent. This means she has to know everyone's job. When Stacey left, Dawn became treasurer for awhile. She was more than happy to give that job back since she hates math.

Besides scheduling appointments, taking dues, and discussing how to spend the dues (if any money is left over we get to do something fun like have a pizza party), we also write in our club notebook. (Guess who's great idea this was! You got it.)

In the notebook we write about our baby-sitting experiences. It's a great resource. If you're baby-sitting for kids you don't know, you can just check the notebook and find out about them. It also gives you ideas on how other members have solved particular baby-sitting problems.

So, you can see that even if the phone never rang, we'd be plenty busy fitting all this into a half hour. But, today the phone was ringing like mad. We'd all taken jobs when Mrs. Newton called at five minutes to six. She needed someone to take care of four-year-old Jamie and little Lucy the next night.

"Nobody's free," said Mary Anne after checking the record book. "We'll have to call Shannon."

Everyone looked at Kristy. She's usually the one to call Shannon since they're friends. Today Kristy cringed slightly. "Could somebody else call her?" she asked sheepishly.

"What's the matter?" asked Dawn.

"Lately Shannon's been calling me asking if I want to go out and do things with her," Kristy explained. "Her schedule has changed and she has more time on her hands. It seems her school friends are busy with other things."

"Shannon's nice," said Stacey. "Don't you want to hang out with her?"

"Who has the time to hang out?" Kristy cried. "It's nothing against Shannon. It's just that with baby-sitting and the club meetings and other stuff, I don't have any time. Whenever Shannon calls I have to say no because I really am busy. I don't want to hurt her feelings, but I think they're getting hurt just the same."

"Tell her to call *us*," Stacey said. "I think Shannon's cool."

"Me, too," agreed Claudia.

"Yeah?" Kristy said, her face brightening. "Then I *will* call her. I'll ask her about the job and tell her to get in touch with you guys about doing things together."

"I've always wanted to know Shannon better," said Dawn.

Kristy punched in Shannon's phone number. "Great," she said with a smile. "Another problem solved."

CHAPTER 3

"Hi," Mme Dupre greeted the volunteers. We'd assembled outside Mme Noelle's classroom. Besides Mary and me there were four other volunteers from different ballet classes. Two of them were boys.

Mme Dupre is French like Mme Noelle, but she's much younger — somewhere in her twenties — and her accent isn't nearly as thick. She's kind of pretty, with grayish-blue eyes and a high forehead. She wears her long brown hair swept back off her face in a tight ponytail. Normally she assists Mme Noelle, but I guess she'd been excused so she could conduct this special class.

Today, instead of her usual black outfit, she wore gray tights, a matching leotard, bright warm-up leggings, and a red dance skirt. She must have noticed me looking at her. "On Tuesdays from now on, you can wear more casual work-out clothing," she told us. "I think it might put the children at ease since they haven't been in a dance class before."

"All right!" I cheered happily. Sometimes I get tired of wearing the same old black leotard all the time.

Mme Dupre smiled at me. "The kids are already in the practice room down the hall. Let's go see what we can do with them."

"I can't believe Vince Parsons volunteered," Mary whispered to me as we walked down the hallway. She nodded toward the boys who were up ahead beside Mme Dupre.

"Which one is he?" I whispered back.

"He's the snobby-looking one," she replied. I knew who she meant immediately. Of the two boys, one was Latino, with olive skin, and very handsome. The other was thin with tight blond curls, a long narrow nose, and super-straight posture. "Snobby" perfectly described the expression on his face.

"Is he really a snob?" I asked.

"The worst," Mary said. "He goes to my school and you'd think he was already a major dance star instead of a student. The other guy is cute, though. I don't know him, but I'm going to try hard to change that!"

"Do you know either of the girls?" I asked, referring to the other volunteers who were hurrying along with us.

"The redhead is named Darcy," Mary told me. "I don't know the dark-haired girl."

When we reached the large practice room it was in an uproar. Screaming, shouting kids were running in all directions. I saw almost forty boys and girls, most of whom looked about eight or nine years old. Mary and I glanced at one another nervously. It seemed doubtful that Mme Dupre would be able to quiet them down, never mind teaching them to dance.

Mme Dupre turned off the bright overhead lights. Since it was winter time, the sun was already setting and the room became quite dark. She clapped her hands sharply. "Please space yourselves and find a seat on the floor," she said loudly.

The kids settled down quickly. Madame turned the lights back on and strode to the center of the room. "Welcome students," she said. "How many of you have studied dance before?"

The students looked at one another but no one raised a hand. "I can do the funky chicken!" yelled a boy with a mop of dark curls and big brown eyes. He got up, tucked his arms in, and began to prance around the room, bobbing his head and flapping his arms. Of course, the class broke into peals of laughter. Even I bit my lip to keep from smiling.

"Very nice," Mme Dupre said tolerantly. "And what is your name?"

"Devon Ramirez."

"Thank you, Devon. You may sit down now," said Mme Dupre. "Has anyone else taken classes?"

One little girl with very dark skin nodded shyly. Mme Dupre noticed her. "What classes have you taken?" she asked.

The girl spoke so quietly that I couldn't hear her, even though she was in the front. "Please speak up," Madame prodded gently.

The girl's dark eyes grew large, as though she felt suddenly trapped. "No, I never took a class," she said in a barely audible voice.

"Oh, all right," said Mme Dupre. "Well, I'm very pleased that none of you has prior training. We won't have to break any bad habits. Here we will start fresh and learn to do things the right way." She stretched out her arms toward us volunteers. "I want you to meet Mary and Jessi. They're on my left. And Vince, Raul, Darcy, and Sue are on my right. They will be helping me. My name is Mme Dupre."

"Hey, like Jazzy Jo Dupre and the Fly Boys!" cried a pudgy blonde girl with large green eyes. "Man! Now those guys are super cool! Will we learn to dance as good as them?"

"Ballet is a good basis for all dance," Mme

30

Dupre replied. "All right, class. We will begin with basic warm-ups. Stay seated, and put your legs out straight in front of you. I want you to bend forward slowly and touch your toes."

"This is like gym!" Devon Ramirez complained. "I thought we were supposed to be dancing."

"You must always warm up before dancing," Mme Dupre told him. "Touch your toes, please."

"All right, but this isn't what I thought it was going to be," Devon said warily as he bent forward.

When the whole class was bent forward, it was easy to spot two girls busily whispering together in the back. They sat side by side and seemed totally unaware of what was going on in the rest of the class. "Jessi, please go back and speak to those girls," Madame instructed me.

The girls were so engrossed in their conversation that they didn't even see me coming. One was petite with lots of red curls. The other had long, limp blonde hair and porcelain-white skin. When I was nearly on top of them, they looked up at me. "You're supposed to be warming up like the rest of the class," I said pleasantly.

"Oh, that's all right," said the redhead. "We

don't really belong here. Our mothers made us come. You can just ignore us."

I hadn't expected that reply! "Well, as long as you *are* here, why don't you join in?" I suggested.

"No, we'd rather not," said the blonde matter-of-factly.

I glanced up to the front of the room and saw Mme Dupre watching me. Now what? I thought. "We'd really like for everyone to co-operate," I said.

"Don't mind us a bit," said the redhead, in a tone that was oddly old-sounding. "You attend to the others. We'll be fine."

I suddenly thought of those mothers I some-times see shrieking at their kids in the super-market. "You have to do it because I said so!" they yell. When I see them I say to myself, I'll never be like them. But suddenly I understood how those mothers might be feeling.

"Please join the class," I begged.

Just then, I noticed Mme Dupre approach-ing. "Ladies, if you can not participate, please go out in the hallway," she said in a no-nonsense voice.

The girls looked at one another. "Will you tell our mothers?" the blonde asked.

"Your mothers will be told not to send you back to class next Tuesday, yes," replied Mme Dupre.

The next thing I knew, the girls had moved apart and were touching their toes. "Jessi, walk among the children and make sure they are in the correct position," she instructed me. I was glad I didn't hear a hint of criticism in her voice because already I felt badly about having failed at my first official volunteer assignment.

After the warm-up exercises, Madame put on a tape of the musical score from the movie *Fantasia*, and told the kids to move to the music. Watching them was a riot. Some of them were out-and-out silly. Others were so deadly serious that it was just as comical.

Madame gave us volunteers the job of walking around, asking each kid his or her name, then writing it down and rating them as dancers on a scale of one to five. Five was to mean "lots of natural potential," and one was to mean that the child seemed stiff and offbeat. Two, three, and four were somewhere in the middle. "Don't worry if you overlap and observe the same children," she told us. "I'll put all the results together tonight, and I like to have more than one opinion."

As I walked through the room with my paper and pencil, I decided that most of the kids fell into the two, three, and four ratings. There were a few exceptions, though. For example, the kid named Devon was being seriously silly — twirling around with his arms held out wide so that he batted other kids out of the way. Still, something in the way he moved with the music made me rate him a five.

And, surprisingly, the quiet little girl who said she hadn't taken classes (her name was Martha) appeared to have some mastery of basic ballet steps and a lot of grace. She got a five from me, too.

The two whispering friends (the redhead was Nora and the blonde was Jane) just sort of bobbed up and down as they talked. I gave them both a one.

The plump, blonde fan of Jazzy Jo Dupre and the Fly Boys (who was named Yvonne) had a hilarious style which consisted of bouncing around wildly, her head shaking and her hair flying everywhere. I just had to rate her a five, too.

The time zoomed by. Before I knew it, parents started to gather in the doorway to pick up their kids. For the first time that day, I became aware that these were very underprivileged people.

The kids seemed so high-spirited and happy that I hadn't thought of them as "underprivileged." Now something in the parents' faces reminded me of that. Even though a lot of them were dressed neatly and smiled as they watched the end of class, something in their eyes was different from what I see in the eyes of the parents picking up their kids at Stoneybrook Middle School. Was it sorrow? Tiredness? A bit of both? It was hard to describe, but it was definitely there.

It made me sad.

And then it made me glad I'd volunteered to help teach the class.

We handed our evaluation sheets to Mme Dupre as the kids left the room. She thanked us and said we'd all been very helpful.

"That was fun, wasn't it?" Mary said to me.

"It was," I agreed. "Some of those kids are real characters."

We began walking toward the dressing room. "But whatever on earth is Mme Dupre going to do with all those kids?" Mary wondered.

"I know what you mean. Is she just going to let them dance around for an hour and a half every day?" I replied. "They won't learn much that way."

"I guess we'll have to wait and see," Mary said.

In the dressing room we met up with the rest of our regular class. "How did it go?" asked Katie Beth.

"It was an experience," I said, laughing.

She gave a snort. "I'll bet! An experience I could live without."

"No, it was fun, really."

As I spoke to Katie Beth, I noticed Mary taking off her leotard. She frowned as she gazed into the mirror. "I am getting to be such a pudge," she fretted.

"You definitely have a few pounds to lose," said Mindy Howard as she joined the conversation. "Get them off and you'll see how much easier it is to do those jumps. Don't you think that's true, Jessi?"

"I don't know. I never really — " I began. But just then Carrie came into the dressing room.

"So? Were the kids total monsters?" she asked.

"No, but we sure have our work cut out for us," I replied.

Mary laughed. "You can say that again!"

CHAPTER 4

Thursday

I had my hands full when I sat for the Papadakises today after school. Not only did I wind up sitting for Sari, Linny, and Hannie, but Karen (Brewer) and Nancy Dawes came over, too. Hannie, Nancy, and Karen sure are the Three Musketeers. When they get together, everyone's imagination starts running wild!

Kristy hadn't bargained for two extra kids when she went to her job at the Papadakises'. But she didn't really mind finding Nancy and Karen there playing with Hannie. Since Karen is her stepsister, Kristy was glad to see her. And she knows Nancy very well. The three girls are all seven years old and are practically inseparable, which is why they call themselves the Three Musketeers.

The Papadakises live right across the street from Kristy, so she's the one who usually takes the jobs with them. That day, when Kristy arrived, the kids were already in the middle of a game called "Let's All Come In." It's a making-believe, dress-up game which is supposed to take place in a hotel. As soon as Kristy shut the door behind Mrs. Papadakis they swept her right into their play.

"Hurray!" cried Hannie. "Now Sari doesn't have to be the Bill Capstin anymore." (She meant bell captain.) Kristy laughed when she saw Sari, who is just two, propped up on pillows behind the coffee table. The older girls had plopped a big captain's hat on her head — I guess to make her look official. Sari was busy scribbling on a pad (which was supposed to be the hotel registration book).

Karen plucked the cap from Sari's head.

"Here," she said, handing the cap to Kristy. "Sari was filling in for you, but she's not too good at this game. All she does is mess up the sign-in book and ring the hotel bell."

As if Karen's words had reminded her, Sari began smacking the call bell on the coffee table and shouting, "Bell! Bell! Bell!"

"See what I mean?" said Karen.

"Well, I'm here to take over now," said Kristy as she sat behind the coffee table. "Sari can be my assistant."

Kristy looked around at the kids who were all dressed in costumes. Karen wore a purple satin robe over her regular clothing. Her eyes were smudged with dark eyeshadow and her hair was teased up like a fright-wig. Hannie wore a small hat with a veil, a pair of her mother's shoes, and a lace shawl. Nancy had clipped a long fake blonde braid to her brown hair, and was wearing lots of red lipstick. A length of white tulle was wrapped around her shoulders. "Who's at the hotel today?" Kristy asked.

"Nobody yet," Nancy told her. "We're starting all over now that you're here."

"I see the bellhop is on the job," Kristy noted.

Nine-year-old Linny (who is a boy, by the way) was dressed in his father's oversized blazer. "I don't want to be the bellhop, Kristy," he complained. "They said I have to. Do I?"

"Why don't you let him be something else?" Kristy suggested to the girls.

"Then who will carry the suitcases?" Hannie asked.

"You don't have any suitcases!" Linny shouted.

"Pretend suitcases!" Hannie shouted back. "Don't you know this is a pretend game?"

"I don't want to stand around and carry air," Linny insisted.

"Here's an idea," Kristy interrupted. "Linny, why don't you be the bellhop for the girls, and then you can check in as someone else after they're done."

"Okay, I guess," Linny agreed sulkily.

With that crisis solved, the game began. Karen was the first to check in. She stooped over and looked about warily as she pounded on the call bell. "Yes, can I help you?" Kristy asked.

"Don't you know who I am?" Karen replied in a crackly voice.

"Oh, now I do!" Kristy cried. "It's you, Mrs. Mysterious. You look a little different than usual."

Karen leaned across the desk to Kristy. "Hannie doesn't have as good costume stuff as Daddy has at his house," she whispered seriously. "I did the best I could."

"You look great," Kristy whispered back.

Karen resumed her Mrs. Mysterious character (which is her favorite person to be in this game). "I'm all worn out," she sighed. "I have just come from meeting with the Addams Family. That family is a scream, if you know what I mean."

"I can imagine," Kristy replied. "How did your meeting go?"

Karen smiled. "It was wonderful. Morticia served us deviled eggs and finger sandwiches for lunch. The fingernails were very crunchy!"

"Eeeewwww!" Hannie and Nancy giggled together.

"Sign in here," Kristy said, turning to a fresh page in the notebook.

Karen bent over the book and scratched in a large X on the top line. She turned to Linny. "Bellhop, there are my lizard-skin bags," she said, pointing to imaginary suitcases.

Linny sighed and flapped the dangling sleeves of his long jacket as he trudged over to where Karen pointed. He pretended to pick up two suitcases. Then he headed for the stairway.

"Bellhop!" Karen shouted in her Mrs. Mysterious voice.

"What?" Linny asked, annoyed.

"You forgot a bag."

Rolling his eyes, Linny went back for the third imaginary lizard-skin suitcase.

Just then, the doorbell rang. "Time out," said Kristy, pulling herself up from her seat. She ran to the front door and pushed aside the long curtain covering the narrow, full-length window next to the door. A girl with short curly blonde hair, big blue eyes, and a ski-jump nose stood outside. It was Shannon Kilbourne.

"Hi," Kristy said, opening the door for her.

"I stopped by your house and your grandmother told me you were over here," she explained as she stepped into the hall.

"What's up?" Kristy asked.

Shannon shrugged. "Nothing. I just wanted to say hi and maybe hang out. If that's okay?"

"Sure," said Kristy. "As long as you don't mind checking into the weirdest hotel on earth."

"What do you mean?" asked Shannon.

"Come on, you'll see," Kristy replied. When they returned to the living room, Sari was once again banging on the bell and Linny stood, pouting, with the jacket thrown on the floor. The girls didn't look too happy, either.

"Linny says he won't be the bellhop," Hannie told Kristy.

"No problem," Kristy said. "I went to the

42

employment agency and got a new bellhop. This is Shannon the bellhop."

Shannon cast Kristy a confused look, but she played along. "Is this my uniform?" she asked, pointing to the rumpled jacket.

"Yes, it is," said Kristy as she sat down behind the coffee table again. "Once you put it on, you will be entrusted with the suitcases of our honored guests. Is that okay?"

"No problem," said Shannon, putting on the jacket.

Immediately, Linny's face brightened and he ran up the stairs. "Be right back," he called over his shoulder.

"Who is our next guest?" asked Kristy.

"Make her stop ringing the bell," said Hannie, pointing to Sari.

Kristy pulled a sheet from the sign-in book. "Here, Sari, draw on this awhile," she said. Luckily, Sari took the suggestion and lost interest in the bell.

When Hannie approached the desk, Kristy recognized her character since it's the one she usually plays. "Ah, Mrs. Noswimple! What brings you here today?"

"Why, my Rolls Royce brought me, of course," answered Hannie. "I am on my way to visit Baron Von-von-von-von and his wife the Red Queen."

"Can a baron marry a queen?" Kristy asked.

"Of course," answered Hannie in her haughtiest voice. "It happens all the time nowadays." Hannie turned to Shannon. "Bellhop, I'll need my ballgown puffed up for tonight. See to it, will you?"

Shannon made a small bow and tried hard not to laugh. "Right away, madame."

After Mrs. Noswimple checked in and Shannon picked up her bags, Nancy entered the room. She was Princess Veronica from the land of Harmonica. This was a brand-new character. Princess Veronica was apparently in flight from an evil wizard who insisted she play the harmonica all day and all night. "My cheeks hurt, my mouth gets dry, my face is all puffy. It's horrible!" she confided to Kristy the bell captain.

As the princess was signing in, a tremendous blast of music made everyone turn to the stairs. Linny came bounding down wearing sunglasses, a black T-shirt, and a red bandana wrapped around his head pirate-style. Heavy rock was blaring from his portable tape player.

He leaped from the bottom step and spread his arms wide. "It's me, Johnny Rocket!" he exclaimed. "I'm bringing my rocking dance fever to your hotel!" He boogied to the center of the room, swinging his tape player as he jumped around like some sort of demented rock star.

The girls caught the "dance fever" right away. Kristy and Shannon burst out laughing at the sight of the kids bopping around in their costumes, legs flailing and arms swinging in time to the pounding beat. Even Sari rocked rhythmically from side to side along with them.

"I guess they don't need us anymore," Kristy said to Shannon, shouting over the loud music.

"I guess not," Shannon agreed.

"Did you get a chance to call Stacey or Dawn or anybody?" Kristy shouted.

"Yeah," Shannon replied with a smile. "I'm meeting Stacey and Claudia downtown on Saturday. Dawn might come, too."

At that moment, Sari tumbled over and started to cry. Kristy hurried to her and snatched her away from the gyrating dancers. "Gee, nobody told me about it," Kristy said, rubbing Sari's back soothingly.

"We just assumed you were busy," Shannon told her. "Do you want to come?"

Kristy sat on the couch and held Sari in her lap. "I can't. I'm baby-sitting on Saturday."

"You can join us another time," Shannon said.

"Yeah, I guess so," replied Kristy. "Another time."

CHAPTER 5

On Friday, I was glad to get to my dance class. I was used to attending twice a week and discovered I missed having that second class. My muscles hadn't tightened up, and I hadn't forgotten anything. But still, I suddenly understood why more girls hadn't volunteered to help Mme Dupre. Missing class made them a bit anxious.

My own anxious feelings surprised me as I stood *pliéing* (that's "plee-ay-ing") at the *barre*. I'd thought I didn't care about falling behind, but I guess I'm more competitive than I'd realized.

Really, though, I didn't have to worry. Once class began I saw that I hadn't missed much, and I danced the same as always.

Well, almost the same.

One time I teetered during my *arabesque* and I misstepped on a simple *assemble* at the end of class. (That's a basic jump.)

I didn't mess up because I'd missed Tuesday's class, though. I messed up because I wasn't completely concentrating on my dancing. I kept watching Mary Bramstedt.

Ever since Tuesday in the dressing room, I couldn't quite get Mary and her diet out of my mind. Something about that bothered me, though I couldn't pinpoint what it was.

Now I was noticing a lot of things about Mary that I hadn't been aware of before. For example, she constantly checked her image in the ceiling-to-floor mirror which took up the entire wall opposite the *barre*.

Okay, all dancers do that. That's what the mirror is there for — so we can check that we are standing straight and in the right position and so forth. But it was different with Mary. She would study herself when she was in line waiting to dance, or during breaks.

You might be thinking, "Oh, how conceited of her," but it wasn't vanity. She didn't seem to be admiring herself. She seemed to be worrying about her appearance. I noticed that she was constantly pinching her waist and her stomach.

After class that day, one of the other volunteers, the redhead named Darcy, waited out in the hall. "Jessi, Mary," she called to us as we filed out.

"Hi," I said, a little surprised. After all, I'd never spoken to Darcy before.

"Listen," she said. "Sue and I were talking with Vince and Raul and we decided to go out for a bite after class next Tuesday. We figured us volunteers should get to know one another. Do you want to come?"

"Sure," I said. I probably answered a little too quickly, but no one at dance school had ever asked me to do anything with them. I was kind of flattered.

"Where are you going?" Mary asked.

"We figured we'd go to the Burger King on the corner," Darcy told her.

"I don't know." Mary hesitated. "That's not the kind of food I usually eat."

"None of us does. At least, not very often," said Darcy. "But it's the closest place and it's cold out. One time won't kill you."

"I suppose." Mary gave in, still sounding doubtful. "One time would probably be all right."

I could tell Darcy was put off by Mary's lack of enthusiasm. "Well, come if you want. You're invited," she said. "See ya Tuesday."

Darcy waved as she hurried down the hall. "It will be good to get to know the other volunteers, don't you think?" I said to Mary.

"I already know Vince and he's no prize," Mary grumbled.

"What about Raul? I thought you wanted to get to know him better," I reminded her.

"What chance do I have with Darcy around? She's so pretty and there's not a drop of fat anywhere on her."

"There's not a drop of fat on you, either," I pointed out.

Mary laughed bitterly. "Don't I wish."

I didn't have any more time to talk. It was Friday — and that meant I needed to get my *derrière* into high gear. (*Derrière* is French for behind.) I had to do my amazing Friday sprint to the BSC meeting.

Once again I managed to slide into the meeting on time. Aside from hearing about Kristy's funny day with the Papadakises, the meeting was pretty quiet. (Kristy seemed unusually quiet, too, come to think of it. I wondered if something was on her mind.)

I didn't take any baby-sitting jobs at that meeting and the weekend turned out to be mostly boring. I didn't mind, though. I was really looking forward to going to Burger King on Tuesday.

Usually I'm not super fashion conscious, but I found myself thinking about clothing. Since I would be free from my regular leotard on Tuesday, I had to decide what to wear. After a lot of thought, I settled on a neon-green leotard and a pair of deep blue work-out pants with heavy yellow slouchy socks. It was important to me not to look babyish. Even though I was younger than the other volunteers, I wanted them to think of me as their age.

That Tuesday, the kids' class was a zoo once again. There were simply too many kids in the class. At least that was my opinion. But Mme Dupre calmly divided the class into six groups and assigned each volunteer to one group.

I was glad when she gave Raul the group which included Devon Ramirez and two of his buddies. I certainly didn't want to have to keep them in line. But I got stuck with Nora and Jane. Those two were determined not to participate any more than was absolutely required. When we worked on *pliés* they bent their knees so slightly you'd think they were little old ladies instead of eight-year-olds. (However, from the corner of my eye, I saw Devon bouncing up and down as if he had springs on his feet. I guess I preferred Nora and Jane — in a way.)

Mary was working with the group that included the shy girl named Martha. (That day Mary wore a big white shirt and a pair of gray sweats. You couldn't tell what her body looked like in that outfit. Maybe that was why she wore it.) Anyway, Martha didn't look at Mary or anyone the whole time. She kept entirely to herself.

After showing the kids the *pliés*, each volunteer took his or her group to the *barre* to practice. At the *barre*, Mme Dupre showed them how to do a *grand battement*. The kids seemed to like that because swinging their legs up to the *barre* was the first really balletlike thing they had learned.

For the last fifteen minutes of class, Mme Dupre put on the *Fantasia* soundtrack again. She told the kids to dance around using only *pliés* and *grand battements* as the basis for their dance steps. The results were funny. I had to look hard to find a real *plié* or *grand battement* anywhere.

Despite the silly-looking dancing, Mme Dupre appeared very pleased by the time class ended. "First we break them of old habits," she said to us volunteers, "then we rebuild them into ballet dancers."

"If you say so," Darcy whispered under her breath as Mme Dupre walked away.

"What do you mean?" I asked her.

"This is the screwiest teaching method I've ever seen," Darcy commented. "I mean, I was taking class when I was as young as these kids. Younger. And I was never in a class like this."

"Me neither," I admitted. "My classes were much more disciplined."

"Of course they were," said Sue who stood nearby. "I'm not sure what Mme Dupre is getting at."

"I don't think she's taking them seriously," Raul said. "They're just a bunch of poor, minority kids to her."

"A lot of them are white," I reminded him.

"Even so, they're inner city kids, so to her they don't count," he insisted.

"I don't think that's fair," Mary objected in a soft voice. "She's here teaching them, isn't she?"

"I agree," said Vince. "I think we should withhold judgment at this point."

I clamped down on my smile as Mary (who was standing behind him) rolled her eyes. Vince had a particularly superior and old-mannish way of speaking.

"Let's discuss this over burgers," said Darcy, pulling the elastic out of her thick red hair. "I'm starving."

We changed quickly and met in front of the school. It had already grown dark and a bitter wind was blowing. We walked toward the Burger King with our collars turned up and our heads down against the icy blast.

"I don't know about you guys," said Sue as she pushed open the glass-and-metal door to the Burger King, "but I wouldn't want to walk one more step. I'm freezing."

"It *is* frigid," agreed Vince. (Again I had to avoid smiling. Vince just cracked me up.)

I knew I was going to eat supper soon, so I only ordered fries and a Coke. "Maybe that's what I should have," Mary fretted from behind me. "Why did we have to come here, anyway? Everything is loaded with calories."

"Have a salad," I suggested.

"Do you know how fattening salad dressing is?" Mary gasped.

"You don't have to order anything," I said.

Mary's eyes darted over to Raul who was at the head of the line to our right. The attendant was busy loading his tray with a large order of fries, a giant burger, and a huge soda. "No, it would look strange if I didn't order," Mary decided. "I'll have a small fries and a small soda," she told the girl behind the counter.

We sat together at a long table. "I wonder if the groups we worked with today will be our permanent assignments," said Sue, unwrapping her cheeseburger.

"Oh, I hope not," said Vince. "I have that little butterball, Yvonne. No matter what I tell her to do, she bounces. I say, *'plié'*, she bounces. I say 'swing your leg back,' she bounces."

"I'll trade her for do-nothing Nora and her friend, Jane," I said. "They are just *not* interested in the class at all."

"Tell me about it." Darcy laughed. "I was amazed that you got them to do *any*thing. I wouldn't want them in my group."

"How are you doing with Devon?" Mary asked Raul.

Raul held up his hand while he finished chewing. "He thinks he's a smart guy. I can handle him," he answered finally. "If he gets out of line I'll clobber him."

"You can't do that!" Sue objected.

"Yeah, I know," Raul admitted. "I don't really know what to do with him. He's pretty disorderly, too. He distracts the other kids."

"This shouldn't be our problem," said Vince with a french fry poised in his hand. "Mme Dupre is the one in charge."

"That's true," Darcy agreed. She turned to Raul. "Do you really think Mme Dupre doesn't expect anything from these kids? Could that be why she's so loose with the program?"

"I guess so," he said. "I'm not sure."

"Perhaps she shouldn't expect too much," said Vince. "The children are there for fun, not to become ballet dancers."

"They should be given a chance like anybody else," Raul insisted hotly.

"I think they are being given a chance," Mary said.

"Only if this program is done right." Raul shook his head sadly. "Sorry if I seem too

54

sensitive about this. But being a minority you become used to getting a raw deal. You get defensive. Haven't you found that, Jessi?"

"No . . . not especially," I answered slowly. "I mean, I know what you're saying, but that hasn't been my experience. In some ways I've been very lucky."

"Well, I've experienced it and I sure hope that's not what's happening here," he said, biting into his burger.

"It's something to keep an eye out for," I said in a way I thought was very diplomatic.

As I bit into my fry I realized I was having a good time. These kids were talking to me as if I were as old as they were and their equal in every way. I glanced at Mary to see if she was having fun.

All I could read from her expression was nervousness. She'd barely eaten one fry. Instead, she'd broken them in half and was moving them around on her tray. If you weren't paying attention, you might think she'd eaten more than she actually had. Occasionally, she sipped on her soda, but the level hadn't gone down much.

I came up with several reasons why she wasn't eating. Maybe she was nervous. Or maybe she didn't want to spoil her dinner. Or maybe she truly hated fast food. (Dawn would consider eating this kind of food inhuman torture.) Or maybe she was on a diet.

The last reason worried me. It was so out of touch with reality. And here was another puzzling question. Why didn't she just say she wasn't going to eat? No one would have cared. Why try to hide the fact that she wasn't eating?

Before I could worry about it much more, my father walked into the Burger King. I had told him to meet me outside. Nothing against my father. I'm proud of him. But there's nothing like having your father show up to remind everyone that you're only eleven. " 'Bye," I said, quickly gathering up my coat and dance bag. "My . . . uh . . . ride is here."

Everyone waved. "So long, Jessi," said Darcy.

"See you again Tuesday," added Raul.

"Those kids are a bit older than you, aren't they?" said my father as we got into the car. (He is *so* overprotective!)

"Yeah, but they're real nice," I told him. It was true. All of them were nice. Even Vince was okay. And I was especially getting to like Mary. I admired the way she disagreed with Raul, even though she had a crush on him. But I was concerned about Mary's problem with food. I just hoped she was okay.

CHAPTER 6

People are so hard to figure out sometimes. I couldn't understand why Mary was so worried about her looks. And I *really* didn't know what Mme Dupre was thinking.

I couldn't believe that she didn't care about the kids in the class. People in ballet tend to be very intense and serious about whatever they do. Mme Dupre certainly fit into that mold. Her gray eyes were constantly moving, taking in everything. I always had the sense that behind her broad forehead was a brain that was thinking . . . thinking . . . thinking, all the time.

Yet, what the other volunteers said was true. So far, her classes had been very undemanding.

Well, if I thought I was confused before, the next class confused me even more. Mme Dupre suddenly shifted gears.

The first change was that a piano was

wheeled into the room and a pianist I'd never seen before — a man in his twenties — came in with it. Mme Dupre clapped her hands sharply for attention. "This is our pianist, Mr. Jon Tsuji," she announced. "He has volunteered to play for our classes." The man smiled and waved as he took his seat behind the piano.

Then Mme Dupre instructed the class to form the groups they had worked in the week before, but she asked each group to get into a line. "Now we will stretch and warm up," she said.

While Mr. Tsuji played a simple, upbeat piece of music, she led the class in a series of warm-up exercises. When that was done, she began a class on the five basic positions for the feet. We volunteers walked up and down each line helping the students.

I was shocked to see Nora and Jane concentrating on placing their feet correctly. I think Mme Dupre had taken them by surprise. (As she had me.)

On the other hand, Devon was still goofing around. He was doing exaggerated, silly versions of the positions, while crossing his eyes and sticking out his tongue. Of course, all the kids around him were giggling and not paying attention.

"Devon!" Mme Dupre said. "Up front. I

want you to demonstrate the five positions to the class."

Now all eyes were on Devon. With his chin held up defiantly, he came to the front of the class. "First position," said Mme Dupre.

Devon put his feet together with his heels touching.

"No! No!" Madame said. "Toes out. Much further out." (In first position, the feet are completely turned out, like Charlie Chaplin's in his old movies.)

Devon turned his feet out further. "Second position," Mme Dupre demanded.

Devon looked at her helplessly. He'd forgotten how to do that. "Feet apart," Madame snapped.

He pushed his feet apart, but lost the proper out-turned position. "No, not right," said Madame. "I suggest you get back in line and pay better attention."

Casting her an angry glance, Devon returned to his place on line.

Mme Dupre then asked the entire class to go the *barre*. It was really crowded, but for *pliés* it wasn't too bad. (No one was kicking anyone else, at least.) Madame instructed them to do *pliés* in all five positions. These *pliés* give your tendons and all the inside leg muscles a good workout. Kids are naturally very flexible. Still, they were in positions that were strange to them. There was a lot of toppling into one another as they lost their balance. This sometimes had a domino effect as one kid knocked over the next, who knocked over the next, who knocked over the kid beside her.

We volunteers worked hard, pushing feet into the right position and encouraging the students to bend lower, to keep their chins up, and to straighten their postures. Nora and Jane tried to get away with their little old lady *pliés* but Madame came along and gently, but firmly, put her hands on their shoulders and pushed down.

One thing I noticed was that the girl named Martha was doing everything perfectly. Even her arm was stretched out gracefully. "Nice work," Darcy told her. In response, Martha just looked down at her feet, almost as if she'd been scolded.

Raul gave Devon some extra attention, but he seemed determined not to cooperate. The minute Raul walked away, Devon would tug on the long black braid of a girl named Cherisse who stood in front of him. "Hey!" she would cry as she whirled around. Devon would smile angelically and look up to the ceiling. But, as soon as she turned back, he'd tug the braid again.

After a few minutes, Mme Dupre spotted

this. "Devon," she said. "I want you to sit over there by the door."

"I wasn't doing anything," he protested.

"By the door. Now," she said calmly.

Devon did as Madame said, making a face at her when she turned back to the class. The class giggled. I'm pretty sure Mme Dupre knew what he'd done, but she didn't turn around. "Continue, class," she said.

Devon slid sullenly to the floor by the door and watched the class, his arms crossed, his body slumped against the wall. I expected Madame to call him back after a few minutes, but she didn't. She seemed to forget about him altogether as she worked with the class on *demi pliés* in fifth position. ("Demi" means half in French. In fifth position, your feet are so close together you can't bend as much as in the other positions.)

As Vince had said, plump little Yvonne bounced through all the *pliés*. Mme Dupre smiled as she held her shoulders and guided her up and down more slowly. "The bounce is fine, but it must be controlled," she told Yvonne kindly.

I was busy working with a boy named Alphonse when I saw Mary stop and push her bangs back off her forehead. She was flushed and sweaty. She bent forward, resting her hands against her knees.

I left Alphonse and went to her. "What's wrong?" I asked.

"I feel weak. I think I'm getting a virus or something," she answered in a shaky voice.

Mme Dupre joined us. "She feels sick," I told her.

Mary straightened up and stepped back unsteadily. "Could I go home?" she asked Madame.

"Of course," Mme Dupre replied. "Can someone come get you?"

"I'll call my mother," said Mary.

"All right," Madame agreed. "Jessi, stay with her until her mother comes."

I walked Mary to the dressing room. "Do you have a fever?" I asked.

"I don't think so," she said, opening her dance bag. She dressed slowly and had to stop a couple of times to rest. During one of those times she sat there in her underwear holding her head in her hands. I couldn't help but notice that she was even thinner than I had remembered. I could see the outline of her bottom rib clearly.

"Would it help to eat something?" I asked. "I have a bag of potato chips with me."

Mary looked up at me. I was sure she was about to say yes, but instead she shook her head. "I'm not really hungry," she said.

I called Mary's mother for her while she

finished dressing. Then I waited out in the lobby with her until Mrs. Bramstedt arrived.

When I returned to the practice studio, Sue was demonstrating a simple *pas de chat*, while Mr. Tsuji played a lively piece. (I knew that piece. It was the "Dance of the Cats," from Act III of *Sleeping Beauty*, in case you're interested.)

Devon was still in his spot by the door, but the *pas de chat* had caught his interest. He was no longer slumped. Now he sat forward attentively, as if he were trying to memorize the movements.

Mme Dupre let every kid take a turn trying it. Once again, this was like something out of *America's Funniest Home Videos*. But, no matter how incorrect they were, most of the kids threw themselves into the exercise. Yvonne, the bouncer, jumped very high off the ground. And Martha almost got the step right. She had natural talent.

I glanced at Devon. He was watching with his head in his hands. I could tell he was dying to try the exercise.

Nora and Jane had kept moving to the back of the line, until they were the last two left. Then they shuffled through the steps, red with embarrassment.

As Jane was finishing up, Madame approached Devon. "Devon, if you can't behave next week, I will have to ask you not to come back to class anymore," she said in a gentle voice.

Devon's dark eyes grew wide. His jaw dropped but he didn't say anything.

"I can't allow you to distract the rest of the students," Mme Dupre explained. "So, you think about what you'd like to do."

With that, Madame walked back to the rest of the class. Devon looked up at me. "Can she do that?" he asked me skeptically.

I nodded. "This isn't like regular school. They can ask you to leave."

"Yeah, well, who cares," Devon muttered, getting to his feet. "This is dumb, anyway."

By then parents were gathering at the door. The *pas de chat* had left the kids charged with enthusiasm. They ran to their parents, excitedly telling them what they'd done. All but Devon. With his hands jammed in his pockets, he joined a broad-shouldered, dark-haired man in a brown construction jacket. The man put his hand gently around the back of his son's neck and they walked out silently together.

I saw Martha take the hand of a tall, lovely woman with very dark skin. The woman gazed into the practice room. There seemed to be a million questions in her curious eyes. When she noticed me, her brow furrowed. She looked surprised to see me there. For a moment, our eyes met, then she turned and left. I wondered what she was thinking.

Soon all the kids were gone. "Thank you for your help," Mme Dupre said to us with a smile. "And thank you, too, Mr. Tsuji."

The man smiled and gave Madame a small nod as he collected his music sheets.

"Did Mary's mother come?" Mme Dupre asked me.

"Yes, she did," I said.

"Very good. If you will excuse me, I must rush to another appointment," Madame said, gathering up her dance bag.

"What was wrong with Mary?" Raul asked me.

"She didn't look well at all," Vince added.

"She thought she was getting the flu or something," I said. (I'd have to remember to tell Mary that Raul had asked about her.)

"I hope it's not contagious," said Darcy.

I looked at the other volunteers for a moment. I wanted to ask them if they had noticed how thin Mary was getting. Had they noticed that she didn't eat at Burger King? I needed someone else's opinion.

But something stopped me from saying anything. Maybe because the guys were there. Or maybe because I didn't want to sound too gossipy.

"Anybody want to go out to eat again?" Darcy asked the group.

"Sure," I said. "Let me go call my dad."

My father hadn't left his office yet so I was able to catch him. "That works out fine," my dad said. "I needed to finish up something here."

"Could you meet me outside at six?" I asked him.

"What? Are you ashamed of your dear old dad?"

"It's not that," I spoke quietly into the phone. "I just don't want them to think I'm . . . you know . . . young."

"How about if we rendezvous at the front counter," he suggested. "I'll be the guy holding the chocolate shake."

"Dad!" I groaned. "Oh, okay."

I decided it wouldn't be that bad. The kids had seen my father the week before and they'd asked me out again. I was glad they had. I liked being part of this new group. For the first time since I'd started at the ballet school, I felt I really belonged.

CHAPTER 7

I didn't realize it, but I guess I was very quiet during the Friday BSC meeting. I couldn't stop wondering what was wrong with Mary — somehow I knew it was more than a virus.

"Earth to Jessi," said Kristy. "Come in."

"Sorry," I said, smiling.

"What's on your mind, Jessi?" Dawn asked.

"Yeah, you've been a million miles away for the whole meeting," added Stacey.

"I was thinking about a girl in my ballet class," I told them. Then I went on to explain how Mary had started a diet and was getting thinner and thinner. I told them what she'd done in Burger King and how she'd gone home early because she felt weak.

"Could she be anorexic?" Stacey asked after I finished.

"What's that?" I asked.

"It's when someone diets and diets until they get way too thin," Mary Anne said.

"Something about the diet gets out of control. The person thinks she's still fat, even though she's not."

"You guys thought I might be anorexic when we first met," said Stacey. "Remember?"

"Why did they think that?" Mallory asked.

"Because I wouldn't eat sweets. I hadn't told anyone about my diabetes yet."

"I heard of a girl who made herself throw up after every meal so she wouldn't gain weight," said Claudia.

"Oh, yuck! Gross!" cried Dawn.

"Just because a person is thin doesn't mean she's anorexic, though," Kristy mentioned. "Lots of people are naturally thin."

"And dieting isn't necessarily bad, either," added Stacey. "If you do it right and eat healthy foods or just cut out sweets — that's a perfectly okay thing to do. But you should only diet if you really need to and if you talk to a doctor about it first."

"Jessi, are you sure your friend is overdoing it?" Mal asked me.

"Pretty sure," I said, thinking about it as I spoke. "Every time I see her she's much thinner. Shouldn't a weight loss be kind of gradual?"

"Yeah, I guess so," agreed Kristy. "A fast

weight loss is always bad news. It does sound like your friend has a problem."

"I don't get it, though," I said. "Why can't she just look in the mirror and see that she's thin enough?"

My friends shrugged. No one seemed to know the answer to that one. "Beats me," said Kristy.

"I think it's a psychological thing," Dawn said.

"You mean that the person is crazy?" I asked, alarmed.

"No, not crazy," Dawn said. "I'm not really sure how to explain it."

"I have an idea," said Claudia. "I bet the genius has some books on the subject. She's studying psychology in school now." (Janine takes some college classes even though she's only sixteen.)

We went down the hall to Janine's room. Claudia looked around quickly and cracked open Janine's door. "Good, she's not around," she said.

"Why? Doesn't she let you use her books?" Mary Anne asked.

"It's not that," Claudia said as we went into the bedroom. "If we told Janine what we wanted to know, she'd keep us here all night while she explained each little detail. You know how Janine is. She'd tell you the case history of every anorexic who had ever walked the planet."

Claudia pulled three psychology books from Janine's tall bookcase. (Typically, Janine's books are arranged alphabetically, so they were easy to find.) Then we hurried back to Claud's room.

Kristy looked through one book, Dawn went through the other, and Mary Anne thumbed through the third.

"Here's something," said Kristy, juggling the thick book on her lap. "Dieting may begin after a seemingly innocent comment about a girl's figure or weight," she read.

"That happened!" I cried. "Mindy Howard said Mary would be able to jump higher if she lost some weight."

"And that's when she started dieting?" asked Stacey.

"I think so," I said.

Kristy had been reading on silently. "That would fit," she said. "It says here that what starts as a diet gets out of control. The person — who is most often a teenaged girl — becomes obsessed with thinness. She no longer sees herself realistically."

"That's Mary," I said excitedly. "She thinks she's fat, but she's skinny!"

"In my book it says anorexics become secretive about not eating," Dawn said, looking up from her textbook. "It says they may dawdle with their food, pushing it and rearranging it, to divert attention from the fact that they're not eating."

"That's exactly what Mary did in Burger King," I told them. "I couldn't understand it, but this explains it."

"Is she moody and irritable?" Mary Anne asked. "My book says that's one of the signs."

I thought about that. "No, not really," I admitted.

"That's good," said Stacey. "Maybe her problem has just started. If someone does something now, I bet it can be stopped before it gets too bad."

"What happens if she doesn't stop?" Mallory asked.

"The disease can lead to weakness, fatigue, and depression, along with low blood pressure, heart rate, and body temperature," Mary Anne replied. She read on to herself and as she did, her face grew very serious. "This isn't good at all," she added, putting down the book.

"Wow," said Dawn. "Can you imagine starving yourself just for the sake of thinness?"

"No," mumbled Claudia, who had just bitten into a Twinkie. "But I guess girls do it all the time."

"What should I do?" I asked. I was feeling sort of scared and helpless.

"Can you talk to Mary?" Kristy asked.

"I tell her she's not fat, but she doesn't believe me," I said.

"Can you tell one of the ballet teachers what you think?" Mary Anne suggested.

I sighed loudly. "I don't know. If they made her leave ballet class or something like that I'd feel terrible. She'd never forgive me. Maybe she'll get sick of dieting on her own."

"Maybe," said Dawn, sounding doubtful.

"I'd better put these books back," Claudia said, taking them from Kristy, Dawn, and Mary Anne.

Just then, the phone rang. It was Watson Brewer, Kristy's stepfather. And he needed a last-minute sitter that night. (Kristy was going to a basketball game at Bart's school that night!)

Stacey was glad to take the job. "Maybe Shannon will come over and hang out with me," Stacey said.

A strange stiff look came over Kristy's face. "Did you guys have fun downtown?" she asked.

"We had a blast!" said Dawn. "Shannon is really funny. She kept doing these imitations of people as they passed by. They didn't see her, of course, but it was a scream."

"Remember that woman with the fishy

face," Claudia laughed. "And she was dressed in blue and green like a fish, too!"

"Oh, yeah," Stacey said, smiling. "When she walked by Shannon turned to me and went . . ." Stacey sucked in her cheeks and bulged her eyes wide. "I thought I would bust trying not to laugh."

"That sounds a little mean to me," Kristy said, unamused.

"I guess," Dawn said. "But the people didn't see her."

"Just the same," Kristy said huffily.

"Why don't you come to the movies with Dawn and Mary Anne and me tonight?" Claudia suggested to Kristy. "Shannon's coming."

"Oh, that means Shannon can't keep me company," Stacey realized. "Too bad."

"I can't go to the movies," said Kristy. "Don't you remember? I'm going to the basketball game."

Something in her voice made me look at Kristy. I couldn't read her, though. I wondered what was going on with her.

Now Mary *and* Kristy both had me completely confused.

CHAPTER 8

Friday

Here's my baby-sitting tip for the day. Never count on being able to do homework when you're baby-sitting. A little extra studying — maybe. But not homework which __must__ be done. Something will probably come up to keep you from doing it. That's what happened to me tonight when I baby-sat at Kristy's. (Kristy, I give you a lot of credit. This was __not__ an easy sitting job!)

Kristy bounded out the front door just as Stacey was about to ring the doorbell at her house. (Excuse me, her *mansion*.) "Hi," Kristy said cheerfully, zipping up her coat. "I can't really talk because we're already late."

"That's okay, have fun," Stacey said.

"Hi, Stace, 'bye Stace," said Charlie, rushing past. He grabbed Kristy's arm and pulled her along. "Come on, Sam!" he called over his shoulder to his brother.

"Good luck," Kristy shouted to Stacey as Charlie dragged her out the door toward his car in the driveway.

Sam raced down the stairs, but skidded to a stop when he saw Stacey. Sam and Stacey really *like* one another. They're kind of going out, but they're still at that early awkward stage. "Hey, I didn't know you were sitting here tonight," he said.

"Didn't Kristy tell you?" Stacey asked. She wasn't really disappointed that he was going out because she expected it; otherwise Sam would have been baby-sitting. And she was glad to see him, even for only a few minutes.

In the driveway, Charlie leaned on the horn. "I'm coming!" Sam yelled to him. "You'd think the world was going to end if Charlie missed two seconds of his date," he complained.

"Go on," Stacey said, smiling. "We'll talk another time."

"Great," said Sam. "Oh, and don't let the monsters get to you," he added as he ran backward toward the car. "Be brave."

Stacey shut the door just as Kristy's mom came into the front hall wearing a long blue evening dress. "Oh, Stacey!" she gasped, jumping back slightly. "You startled me. I didn't hear the bell ring."

"It didn't," Stacey told her. "I sort of slipped in as the others were racing out."

"Charlie does like to be punctual," Mrs. Brewer said, laughing. (Could he be *more* punctual than Kristy!? Is that even possible?)

Mrs. Brewer led Stacey to the family room. Watson was there with the kids. He looked sharp, dressed in a tuxedo. The Brewers sometimes go to very fancy affairs. I guess millionaires are expected to do that sort of thing.

"Hi, Stacey!" said Karen, who was there for the weekend. Her eyes were bright with excitement. She doesn't often have a baby-sitter who isn't a member of her family. And besides that, she likes Stacey a lot.

"Stacey's here! Stacey's here!" Andrew cried, bouncing around the room. (Kristy says Andrew and Karen are often super wound-up when they first come over for the weekend.)

David Michael was draped across the sofa reading an X-Men comic. "Hi, Stace," he said casually as he flipped the pages. David Michael is just a few months older than Karen, but lately he's been thinking of himself as a "big kid."

Emily Michelle was toddling around the room happily. "Puway! Puway!" she said, lifting up her Raggedy Ann doll to Stacey.

"Very good," said Stacey, although she had no idea at all what Emily was trying to tell her.

"Nannie will probably be home before we are," Mrs. Thomas told Stacey. "She has a bowling tournament tonight. But if her team wins, she may be out late celebrating. At any rate, Kristy or one of the boys should be home by eleven." She gave Stacey the number where she and Watson could be reached, told the kids to be good, and gave them each a hug.

"Behave for Stacey," said Watson as he and Kristy's mom left the room.

"Can we have some soda?" Andrew asked immediately after the Brewers were gone.

"I guess," Stacey replied. "But just one glass. Who else wants soda?" Of course, all the kids did. They trailed after Stacey as she went into the huge country-style kitchen and opened the refrigerator. "There is no soda,"

Stacey told them, surveying the contents of the fridge.

"In the pantry," Karen instructed her.

As soon as Stacey opened the pantry door, David Michael cried out: "There's my Lego building set!"

Looking down, Stacey saw a container of the small colorful plastic blocks dumped on the floor. "I've been looking everywhere for these," said David Michael as he knelt to scoop them back in the container. "How'd they get in here?"

"Puway! Puway!" Emily Michelle said happily.

"Oh, I should have known." David Michael groaned.

Stacey got on her toes to reach a bottle of cola on a high shelf. "What does *puway* mean?" she asked.

"It means 'put away'," Karen explained. "Nannie is trying to teach her to put away her toys."

"Isn't she a little young for that?"

"Nannie doesn't think so," said Karen.

"Yeah, well, she should put away her *own* stuff," grumbled David Michael.

Stacey poured the kids' sodas and they all returned to the family room. They were able to agree on watching *Pete's Dragon* on the cable channel. (Getting kids to agree on a TV show always seems like a minor miracle!)

Emily Michelle wasn't interested in the movie, however. Instead, she amused herself by playing her own version of the game Shark Attack, and toddling around.

The peace only lasted until the end of the program. "Where's the remote control?" asked Andrew. Everyone looked around them but they couldn't find it. "Where could it have gone?" Stacey wondered, checking under the couch.

Just then, Emily Michelle cried out, "Puway!"

"Uh-oh!" David Michael moaned.

They began an all-out search of the family room. Here's what they found: one of Andrew's sneakers in the toy box; Karen's bracelet under a cushion; David Michael's Ninja Turtle action figure behind some books on a bottom shelf; Kristy's address book stuffed between the crack in the couch cushions; and Emily's Raggedy Ann doll sticking out from under a corner of the rug.

Here's what they didn't find: the remote control.

"I'm sure it will turn up," said Stacey. "In the meantime, we can change the channel by hand."

"No!" Karen cried, truly alarmed. "Daddy

says we shouldn't touch the TV. He says we might break something."

"That's just for you little kids," said David Michael. "Stacey and I can touch it."

"I'm only a few months younger than you!" Karen yelled indignantly.

"Well, a few months is a lot," David Michael insisted.

"It is not." Karen pouted. "Nancy and Hannie are almost a year older than me and they don't think I'm a little kid."

While they bickered, Stacey studied the TV. She didn't think Watson would mind if she touched the controls, but the truth was she couldn't quite figure what to do. The set was large and fancy. She didn't want to take a chance on messing anything up. "Let's just watch what comes on next," she suggested.

But it was the news, so Stacey turned off the power. "We can play 'Let's All Come In,' " Karen said.

"No way!" Andrew and David Michael yelled at once.

Finally they settled on a game of hide-and-seek. Stacey and Emily Michelle were a team and somehow wound up always being "It." (In the process of searching, Stacey uncovered a set of keys on a closet floor. "Puway," Emily told her when she picked them up. Stacey was sure *someone* would be glad to have them back.)

Playing such a wild game before bedtime wasn't the best idea in the world. Trying to put the kids to bed was nearly impossible. Emily Michelle wasn't too difficult, but Karen, Andrew, and David Michael could not settle down. Karen bounced on her bed while Andrew and David Michael hurled pillows at her. She punched back the pillows, crying, "You can't hurt the flying pillow-popper-hopper bird!"

This kept up until Stacey collected all the pillows and threatened not to give them back until they settled down.

Stacey read to them from *Winnie the Pooh* for over half an hour before they showed the slightest sign of being sleepy. It was nearly ten when they were finally tucked away in bed.

Even though she was pooped, Stacey wanted to start her math homework. But when she went to the family room to get her book, it wasn't on the coffee table where she'd left it. "Oh, no!" she exclaimed, her shoulders dropping wearily. "I hope it wasn't 'puway.' "

She looked under the table and all around the room. She could only come to one conclusion. Emily Michelle had struck again! Which meant the book could be anywhere.

Stacey tore the room apart. She even checked the refrigerator, in case Emily had stuck it in there while Stacey was checking for the soda. After half an hour of searching, Stacey was stumped. She threw up her arms in despair and plopped down into a chair in the family room.

Suddenly the TV snapped on — full blast.

Stacey screamed and leapt out of the chair, her heart thumping in her chest.

Then she reached under the padded chair cushion. There was the clicker!

Stacey turned the TV off again. At that moment, she caught sight of the corner of her book peeking out from behind a curtain.

She retrieved the book and settled down on the couch. Just as she opened it, the doorbell rang. Nannie must have forgotten her keys, Stacey thought. Maybe those were hers I found. Nannie wasn't at the door, though. Shannon was.

"Hi," Shannon said. "We got back from the movies early and I don't have to be home until eleven, so I figured I'd stop by and keep you company."

Stacey was glad to see her, and she felt it would be rude to tell her she couldn't come in. So she resigned herself to doing her math homework at home.

Shannon told her about the movie they'd seen, a spoof of detective movies. "Claudia and I gave it a thumbs up, but Mary Anne and Dawn said thumbs down," Shannon reported. "They thought it was too silly, but that was exactly why I liked it."

Shannon and Stacey had been talking for about fifteen minutes when Kristy returned. As soon as she saw Shannon in the family room, the smile faded from her face. "I thought you went to the movies," Kristy said, without even saying hello.

"She got home a little early," Stacey explained.

"Oh, wow, and now you're here," Kristy sounded annoyed. "Shannon, are you having a problem at home?"

"No, why?" Shannon asked.

"Because you never want to be there," Kristy said.

Shannon looked embarrassed as she got up from the couch. "I'd better be getting home now," she said. "It's almost eleven."

"Yes," Kristy agreed. "You probably should be getting home."

Kristy didn't make a move to walk Shannon to the door, so Stacey got up and did it. "Is

Kristy mad about something?" Shannon asked Stacey as she pulled on her jacket.

"It does seem that way," Stacey agreed. "I can't imagine what she could be mad about, though."

Stacey said good night to Shannon and returned to the family room. "Is everything okay?" she asked Kristy.

Kristy plopped onto the couch and clicked on the TV. "Everything's fine," she said. But Stacey didn't believe her.

CHAPTER 9

The next week was a pretty average one. But there were two highlights. On Monday I got a letter from my friend Quint. (Actually, he's more than a friend. We really *like* one another, if you know what I mean.) He lives in New York City and studies ballet at the Juilliard School, which is very famous and hard to get into.

I miss him and I love his letters. (Even though it means I then have to write back. I'm not exactly the world's greatest letter writer.)

When I receive a letter from Quint I always write back as soon as possible. This time, at least, I had something very interesting to write about — my classes with Mme Dupre. I told him all about it and asked what he thought of Madame's teaching method. Plus, I told him about Raul's comments and asked what he thought of them. (Quint is also black, so I figured he must have some feelings about what Raul had said about the way minorities are treated.)

Then I told Quint about Mary. "I don't want to tell a teacher what I suspect," I wrote. "It seems disloyal to Mary. But I don't want Mary to get sick. I'd feel awful if I could have stopped her from becoming anorexic and I didn't say anything. What do you think I should do?"

As I sealed the letter in the envelope, I felt a little less anxious about Mary. I knew Quint would have something helpful to say. He always does.

The other highlight of the week was the kids' class, itself. As I got to know the students better, I enjoyed it more and more. There was one sad part, though. Devon didn't show up. I guess he had decided not to come back. "Mme Dupre was too hard on him," said Raul after class.

"But he was disrupting everyone," said Mary. "You can't have it both ways, Raul. First you say she's too easy, then you say she's too hard."

"I guess," Raul admitted. "But I liked the kid."

I had to hand it to Mary. In her own quiet way, she always spoke up and said what she thought — even if it meant disagreeing with a guy she liked.

When I asked Mary if she was feeling better, she claimed she'd only had a twenty-four hour virus. But she still looked pale, and thinner than ever. I didn't have a chance to talk to her beyond that. Madame worked the kids and the volunteers hard, and after class everyone seemed to have to get somewhere.

Guess what. I had found that the only thing I didn't like about the Tuesday class was that it really *did* interfere with my regular Tuesday class. I was shocked at how much I missed that class. So, by Friday, I was totally psyched to get back to work.

Then something terrible happened during class.

We were in the middle of our warm-up *pliés* when Mary fell to the floor. She had fainted!

The entire class crowded around her, but Mme Noelle made us move back. "Someone rush and get ze first aid kit from ze receptionist!" she cried as she knelt beside Mary, patting her pale cheeks gently.

Carrie Steinfeld ran out of the room and returned in a flash with the kit. Madame took a white stick of smelling salts out of the box and waved it under Mary's nose. Mary's eyes fluttered, and she began to cough.

Madame asked for a chair and told Mary to sit on it with her head down between her knees. Just then, Mme Dupre stuck her head into the room. "What's wrong?" she asked.

"Madame, call ze emergency rescue squad, *s'il vous plait*," Mme Noelle said to her.

"No!" Mary cried, her eyes now open wide. She sat up straight. "It's just a virus. I'll be fine. Please."

Another virus? I thought. No way!

Mme Noelle studied Mary, her sharp eyes boring into her. She put her hand on Mary's forehead. "No fever. Are you dizzy now, *mademoiselle*?" she asked.

Mary shook her head. "No, not at all," she replied.

Madame stood up. "Will you ask ze receptionist to call Mary's parents?" she asked Mme Dupre, who was waiting in the doorway. "Someone must come to get her."

"Of course," replied Mme Dupre.

"*Mademoiselle* Bramstedt, I wish you to dress and wait in ze lobby. But do not leave without speaking to me. I wish to talk wiss your fazzer or muzzer."

"I'll go with her," I volunteered quickly. *I* needed to talk to *Mary*, and I couldn't wait a moment longer.

"Yes, a good idea," Madame agreed. "She should not be alone."

Slowly, Mary got to her feet and we left the studio. I didn't say anything until we were alone in the dressing room. Truthfully, I wasn't sure what I was going to say until I opened my mouth.

"Mary, I think you should stop dieting," I said directly.

"What do you know about it? You're just a kid!" Mary snapped at me.

I was stunned. She'd never spoken to me like that before. I remembered that Mary Anne had said moodiness and irritability were a sign of anorexia, so I pushed on. "Do you know what anorexia is?" I asked.

Mary's eyes narrowed angrily. "Yes, I know what it is! And I am not anorexic."

"Maybe not yet, but you're headed in that direction," I said, my voice rising. "You have all the symptoms."

"I didn't know you were a medical authority," Mary scoffed as she slipped out of her leotard. I saw that she was even thinner than the week before.

"My friends and I looked it up in a book."

"Why?" demanded Mary.

"Because I was telling them how worried I am about you."

Mary's hands flew to her thin hips. "You told your friends I have anorexia?" she exploded. "How dare you! Besides, it's a lie."

"Mary, I care about you, and you need help." As the words came out of my mouth, I knew beyond any doubt they were true.

Mary's face went bright red. In a rage, she threw her dance bag against the wall. "This is not your business!" she cried, stepping close to me. "I can handle it myself. Don't you talk to anyone else about this!"

Suddenly, I realized my hands were trembling. No one had ever screamed in my face before. Tears were brimming in my eyes but I fought them back.

As Mary and I stood facing one another, Mme Dupre looked in. "Is there a problem?" she asked, her eyes darting from Mary to me.

"No. No problem," said Mary, quickly going back to her dressing.

Mme Dupre looked at me questioningly, but said nothing.

When she was gone, Mary turned to me. "I'm sorry, Jessi. I've been in a bad mood lately, but it's nothing for you to worry about. Sorry I got so bent out of shape."

"Get some help, Mary," I repeated. "Please?"

She turned her back to me and pulled on her jacket. After that, she ignored me as we walked to the lobby. When we got there a man was speaking with Mme Noelle. I assumed from the resemblance to Mary that he was her father. Both he and Madame seemed very serious.

"I suggested to your fazzer zat you consult

a doctor about zis virus," Mme Noelle told Mary when we approached them.

"I just need to get to bed," Mary said.

"Perhaps some chicken soup," Madame suggested.

Mary nodded. I prayed she'd take Mme Noelle's advice — it was wiser than Madame probably realized.

CHAPTER 10

I smiled as soon as I walked into the kids' class on the following Tuesday. Devon was back!

He stood with two of his pals, laughing, as if he'd never been away.

Maybe he'd just been ill the week before. But I thought something else had happened. Maybe he had decided not to return to class, but then had missed it too much to stay away. Something very subtle had changed about him. For one thing, he wasn't running around the room like a maniac before class.

For that matter, something had changed in all the kids. They no longer seemed as wild as when we'd first met. Now when Mme Dupre walked into class she didn't need to dim the lights. Her presence was enough to quiet the kids down.

Mr. Tsuji began to play a lively melody and

Madame asked me to lead the warm-ups. The kids had come to know the stretching and bending exercises well.

As I worked with the class, I looked over at Mary. Her baggy Tuesday dance wear seemed even baggier. Her eyes appeared larger and her cheekbones higher. I guess getting thinner made her features stand out more. I wondered if she'd been to the doctor as Mme Noelle had suggested. Perhaps a doctor would catch on to what was happening and could talk some sense into Mary.

I hadn't spoken to her since the other day. And today, in the dressing room, she hadn't made eye contact with me even once. I was sure she was avoiding me.

When the warm-ups were finished, Mme Dupre taught the class some small jumps called *échappé* (which means "escape"). These jumps can be done from several ballet positions. Madame asked the kids to stand in second position and jump straight up, pointing their toes, then land again in second position.

The room exploded with thuds as the kids jumped and landed. It seemed to me that even the windows shook.

After awhile Mme Dupre broke the class into groups. These groups were different than the ones they'd been in before. I wasn't surprised to see that Madame had separated Nora from Jane, and that Devon was nowhere near his friends.

Today the kids were really going to learn to do a *pas de chat* correctly. Each of us volunteers was assigned a group. Mary worked with Devon's group. This was a switch because up until this time Mme Dupre had always paired him with Raul. That was Mme Dupre for you, forever watching, making adjustments, and thinking.

Martha was in my group. I couldn't believe how shy she was even after all this time. I never saw her speak to any other kid. She barely even looked at anyone.

But she could dance!

Although a *pas de chat* is one of the first jumps that children learn, I thought it was ambitious of Madame to try to teach it in this class. In a way, I understood why she chose it. It doesn't require a lot of strength, and kids like the idea of a jumping cat. And they love to jump.

A *pas de chat* does require a certain amount of experience, though. At least if you want it to look right.

Which brings me back to Martha. By only her third try, her jump was very close to being exactly right. She was a natural — from the way she held her arms, to her posture, to the way she lifted her chin. And she jumped higher than any of the other kids. "Are you sure you never took lessons?" I asked after she came down lightly from her jump.

"Five," she said in her soft voice.

"What?" I asked.

"I took five lessons once."

"But why did you stop? You're so good."

She smiled, then looked away and shrugged. "I just stopped, that's all."

"Well, you should start again. You have a real gift," I told her.

Martha ducked her head and wouldn't look at me, but she was smiling. It was the very first time I'd seen her smile.

As I worked with the other kids I glanced over to Mary's group — in time to see Devon leap into the air. His movements were way too large and uncontrolled. He had great energy and dramatic flair, though. When he was done, Mary walked him slowly through the proper positions.

It occurred to me that each one had something to offer the other. Devon needed Mary's technical knowledge, and Mary needed some of Devon's fire in her dancing.

What a change in Devon, too. He listened to Mary, absorbing her every word. It was clear he'd made up his mind to get serious.

Class went by so quickly that when the first mother arrived, I thought she had come extra early. She hadn't. It was actually time to leave.

"Wonderful work," Mme Dupre told the class. "I will see you next week."

"Good going, kids," I said to my group. They smiled at me and then headed for the door. "Especially you," I whispered into Martha's ear when the others were a little distance away.

What she did then took me by surprise. She turned and wrapped me in a quick, tight hug. Then she ran off to the doorway where her mother was waiting for her.

Want to hear something funny? I got this big lump in my throat and felt like I was going to cry.

What a weird feeling. I was really happy, but fighting back tears at the same time. Until that moment, only certain parts of some ballets and the end of the movie *It's a Wonderful Life* had made me feel that way. This was the first time real life had given me that crying-happy feeling.

Again, I saw Martha's regal-looking mother staring at me. I wanted to speak to her, but the lump was still in my throat. I wasn't sure I could talk. I looked at the ceiling and tried to pull myself together. When I looked back, Martha and her mother were gone.

"Good class, huh?" said Sue, joining me.

"It sure was," I agreed, clearing my throat.

"Want to go to the King for a snack?" she asked me.

"Yeah, is everyone going?"

"I think so. Hey, Mary," Sue called to her. "Are you coming to Burger King?"

"Thanks, but I can't," Mary said, avoiding my eyes. "I have to go running."

"In this cold weather!" Sue yelped.

"You don't feel it when you run," Mary replied.

"I'd feel it," said Sue, laughing. "See you in the dressing room, Jessi," she told me as she left.

"Aren't you supposed to be taking it easy?" I asked Mary before she could get away from me.

"I'm all better," Mary said. "Stop worrying about me, okay? You sound like my mother and it's really starting to bug me."

"Sorry," I said. "But why don't you come with us?"

"Jessi!" Mary snapped. "Chill out! All right?"

"All right," I said.

"Come on, Jessi," Darcy called to me from the doorway.

"I'm coming," I said, walking away from Mary.

Maybe Mary was right. Maybe I was making a big deal over nothing. Maybe Mary was doing what was necesary to keep her ballet career going, and she didn't need me hassling her about it. Besides, it wasn't my problem or any of my business.

That's what I told myself as I headed for the dressing room. But I didn't believe it.

CHAPTER 11

On Tuesday, when I got home from my class, a letter was waiting for me from Quint. I tore it open, hoping he'd have some advice about Mary.

After a few words about what was happening with him (school, ballet class, that sort of thing) he plunged right into the topic. "Dieting!" he wrote in capital letters. "That's the number one topic among a certain group of girls in my ballet class. It drives me crazy, but I feel sorry for them, too. They think they're under a lot of pressure to look a certain way. It's not half as bad for a guy. In ballet guys don't have to look as uniform as girls. Some girls wind up with only two choices — diet like mad, or drop out. I can't imagine having to make that choice, not after spending my whole life involved in ballet. Those girls wouldn't have to quit dancing altogether, of course. A lot of them go into theatrical dancing, like on Broadway and in traveling shows. Others become teachers."

Quint's letter made me feel better. At least Mary wasn't the only person with this problem. "Weight can be a big problem in dancing," Quint went on. "A lot of people say that the physical standard for ballerinas isn't realistic. If you look at pictures of old-time dancers — ones that were stars — you see that they're not nearly as thin as dancers today. I think the trend now is for dancers to be a little heavier than they have been recently. It's happening slowly, but you *can* notice it when you go to the ballet." (I'm really envious that Quint lives in the city and goes to see the top ballets all the time!) "Maybe if you tell this to Mary, she'll feel better."

I was definitely going to tell that to Mary. If she would talk to me, that was!

"Oh, I had a great idea the other day," Quint wrote in the next paragraph. "You made me think of it when you asked about the minority thing. Yeah, it is rougher if you're a minority. There's no sense saying it's not. And in ballet it's for the same reason that some girls find themselves dieting like crazy. There's this idea that everyone in the corps de ballet should look alike. People used to be (and sometimes still are) afraid to pair a non-white guy with a white ballerina (or vice versa) in a *pas de deux*. That's changing, though. There are non-white dancers in the corps de ballet now, and more and more mixed couples dancing — especially in the modern pieces."

This was all very interesting, but I was getting impatient to hear Quint's great idea. Finally he came to it.

"Here's my idea. Why don't you talk to Mme Dupre about offering a scholarship to a couple of the kids who seem very gifted. They might be white or not, but the point is, they would be kids who otherwise couldn't afford class. The school probably won't go for it, but it's an idea, anyway."

Quint finished his letter with some encouraging thoughts about spring break and how we could arrange to meet. He writes such great letters. This one was a little more formal than most of them, but that might have been because of the serious subject.

His scholarship idea was pretty awesome. Did I have the nerve to suggest it? I wasn't sure. Mama always tells me just to speak up. "The worst that can happen is that someone will say no," she tells me. Which is true. But sometimes shyness gets the best of me. I'm not shy with kids my own age. With adults sometimes my tongue ties up into a knot. I couldn't exactly picture myself walking up to Mme Dupre and suggesting the school donate thousands of dollars worth of scholarship money. Besides, Mme Dupre would probably tell me to discuss it with Mme Noelle. Now there was an intimidating thought! I really didn't think the school would give out scholarships just because an eleven-year-old told them to.

Or would they? I had to think about it some more.

I was folding Quint's letter when the phone rang. "It's for you, Jessi," Aunt Cecelia called from the kitchen. I picked up the extension in the living room.

"Hi," Kristy said. "How's it going?"

"Okay."

"Listen, are you free to sit at my house this Saturday?" she asked. "Or are you going to the fair at Shannon's school, like everybody else?"

"Oh, yeah, they asked me to come but I have some studying to do," I said. "I could sit for a couple of hours, though."

"Good, because I promised to go to a planning meeting at school for the spring dance. I'll only be gone a few hours myself. Can you come over at two?"

"No problem," I said.

"Thanks, 'bye."

" 'Bye." I laid the phone down gently as Aunt Cecelia came in.

"You look pretty faraway," she commented. "What's on your mind?"

"Aunt Cecelia, what would you do if someone you knew was hurting herself and she didn't even realize it?" I asked.

Aunt Cecelia sat on the chair across from me. "Does this have to do with drugs?" she asked.

"No, dieting," I told her. "Too much dieting."

"Hmmm." Aunt Cecelia sat back in the chair thoughtfully. "You might have to tell an adult who knows this person about what's happening with her."

"Isn't that tattling, though?"

"Not if your friend's health is at stake. Doesn't anyone else around her notice this?"

"So far, no one seems to think anything of it," I told her. "My friend is pretty good at hiding it. She pretends to eat and she wears big clothes."

"Are *you* sure there's a problem?" Aunt Cecelia questioned.

I thought about this. "Eighty percent sure," I estimated.

"You have good instincts, Jessi. Go with your gut," said Aunt Cecelia. "I think you should tell someone."

"Thanks. That's what I was thinking. I was just hoping there was another way."

"There's an expression," said Aunt Cecelia. "You have to be cruel to be kind."

"What does that mean?" I asked.

"It means that the best thing to do for a person you care about isn't always the easiest thing. It might even make the person mad at you."

"Oh, it will!" I assured her. "She will be super mad at me. That's for sure."

"Someday she'll realize you were being a true friend," said Aunt Cecelia.

"I hope so," I replied. Somehow I had my doubts about *that*.

CHAPTER 12

Usualy I have to take a deap breth wensday before I go sit for the Kermans. Those kids relly nock me out. This afternoon, thogh the Papadakis kids came over and so did David Micheal! What a crowd! And then Shannon came by with her sisters Tifany, and Maria. But, at leest Shannon was there to help me. We wound up having a ball— a snow ball!

Snow! That was the good news when Claudia sat for the Kormans before our Wednesday BSC meeting. The Korman kids have lots of energy, so taking them outside to play in the snow is a terrific way to keep them busy (and also tire them out a little).

They were already bundled up and ready when Claudia arrived. One-and-a-half-year-old Skylar was so excited about going out that she didn't even cry when Mrs. Korman left. (She did yell, "Mommy!" and look pitiful for awhile, but that's *much* better than usual.)

Snow had been falling all day. Now it was just flurrying and almost four inches of crisp, feathery snow lay on the ground — the perfect kind for packing.

Nine-year-old Bill and seven-year-old Melody immediately began rolling a ball for a snowman in their large front yard. (The Kormans live in Kristy's neighborhood where the houses all have huge front and back yards.) They hadn't gotten very far when a snowball came skidding past them.

"War!" Bill cried gleefully as he began packing a snowball for his retaliation on this unseen attacker.

Linny and Hannie Papadakis came laughing into the yard, their arms loaded with snowballs. Linny and Bill didn't waste a minute. They began bombarding one another with snowballs, ducking and shouting all the while.

"Hey! Hey! Be careful," Claudia cautioned, half laughing as a snowball flew past her shoulder.

"Ow!" Melody cried. A snowball had hit her smack in the chest.

"Take this!" yelled Hannie, hurling a snowball at Linny. Her snowball flew high into the air and crumbled before it dropped to the ground. Hannie isn't exactly the world's greatest snowball maker, or much of a pitcher.

"Girls against boys!" Bill cried, joining forces with Linny. They lobbed a hail of snowballs at the girls, packing them as quickly as they threw them.

Melody and Hannie knew a losing battle when they saw one. They fought back for about two minutes and then ran for cover behind Claudia. "No fair!" Claudia protested as she held up her arms to ward off the shower of snowballs the boys were now directing her way. "I'm not a human fort."

"Are you building a fort?" cried eight-year-old Maria Kilbourne who had come running into the yard. "Can I help? I'm good at it!"

"That's a great idea," said Claudia as a snowball flew past her ear.

The snowball hit Maria's shoulder. "That's enough," Claudia told the guys. "You win. We quit."

"Ah, come on, don't be chicken!" Bill cried.

"Someone's going to get hurt," Claudia insisted firmly. "Help us make a snow fort, instead."

At that moment, Shannon and her eleven-year-old sister, Tiffany, ran into the yard behind Maria. "What is this? The winter fun headquarters?" Shannon asked with a smile.

"It's turning out that way," Claud replied. "Are you up for building a snow fort?"

"Sure."

Shannon and Tiffany joined the others who were packing snow into four walls. Then they dug out a small doorway and some peek-hole windows. "Now what?" Melody asked, when that was done.

"Let's have another snowball fight," Linny suggested. "You can stay in the fort and pack snowballs while Bill and I sneak up on you."

"Not!" called out Maria.

"Yeah, that's a crummy idea," agreed Hannie. "We're not going to sit inside a fort and let you cream us with snowballs. That doesn't sound like much fun."

"We should do something special," Claudia said, thinking hard. "There probably won't be too many more winter days with as much snow as this one." Her eyes lit with an idea. "Why don't we make a snow village?" she suggested.

"A what?" Hannie asked.

"We'll sculpt a village out of snow," Claud explained.

"Can we drive trucks and stuff through it?" Linny wanted to know.

"Why not?" Claudia said. "We can do whatever we want."

"Cool!" said Melody. "Let's do it."

The kids set to work building the snow village of their dreams. Shannon built a block of shops while Claudia sculpted a big old-fashioned church.

Melody and Hannie built a ranch and then Melody ran inside and came out with an armload of plastic ponies and horses. "Whoever heard of a horse ranch next to a church?" Shannon asked as they lined up the ponies in the corral.

"In the church they pray and at the ranch they pray-ey-ey-ey," said Hannie neighing like a horse.

"This is turning into a very interesting village," said Claudia. It was, too. The boys had built a multilevel garage and stocked it with Bill's Matchbox cars and trucks. Maria had contributed a haunted house complete with a tall round tower and a front porch. And even

Skylar had built a mound of snow.

"That mound is the local ski mountain," Shannon suggested. "This is a haunted, western, ski resort with a magnificent cathedral and excellent parking."

"And horseback riding," added Hannie.

"What more could anyone ask for?" asked Claudia.

"I know what it needs," said Shannon. "A luxury condo for all the movie stars who come here."

"You're right," Claudia agreed. "It has to have a big pool with a chic club next to it."

Shannon and Claudia started piling up snow to build their condo. After a moment, they realized the tower tilted decidedly to the left. "This looks more like the leaning condo of Pisa." Shannon giggled at their crooked tower.

"Only crooked people can come here," Claudia replied. "Thieves and con artists."

"Then we need a jail!" Linny cried excitedly.

"And a police station," added Bill. The boys began creating two square buildings out of snow.

Shannon eyed the leaning condo. "Maybe we can straighten this thing out."

They were laughing over the condo when they saw Kristy across the street. Her face clouded into a frown as she caught sight of them working on their village.

"Hi!" Claud called to her.

Kristy walked into the yard. "What are you guys doing?" she asked.

"Isn't it obvious?" Shannon said cheerfully. "We're building the snow village of the future."

"Oh, I see. Very nice." Kristy's eyes went from Claudia to Shannon and back again.

"Have you got any ideas for our village?" Shannon asked.

"No," Kristy replied.

That's when the alarm bells began ringing in Claudia's head. Kristy didn't have an idea? No way! Kristy always has ideas — about everything. And she just about always volunteered them, whether she was asked or not.

Claudia knew something was wrong.

Shannon must have, too. Because when Kristy turned to leave without even saying good-bye, Shannon ran after her.

Claudia watched for a moment as they talked heatedly out on the sidewalk. "Would you keep an eye on Skylar?" she asked Tiffany. Then she followed Shannon and Kristy. She reached them in time to hear Shannon say, "I want to know why you've been so rude to me. Don't tell me I'm imagining it. I'm not."

"All right, if you want the truth." Kristy spoke angrily. "You wouldn't know anything about the BSC or my friends if it weren't for me."

"Yeah? So?"

"So I don't need you coming around trying to take my place and steal my friends!" Kristy blurted out, her face turning a deep red.

Shannon's jaw dropped. "Steal your . . . I never . . . I . . ."

"Kristy, I don't think that's fair," Claudia spoke up.

"You wouldn't!" Kristy snapped.

"What's that supposed to mean?" asked Claudia indignantly.

"It means that now that everyone is Shannon's friend I'd expect you to stick up for her!"

Claudia was stunned. "I'm still your friend. All of us are still your friends," she said.

"Yeah? Well, lately it sure doesn't feel that way." Kristy bit her lip. Then she stormed across the street.

CHAPTER 13

As you might imagine, the BSC meeting that Wednesday was a little tense. I didn't know what had happened between Kristy, Claudia, and Shannon until Mallory called and told me later that night. (Mal had talked to Mary Anne who had talked to Dawn who had heard what happened from Stacey. Who, of course, got it from Claudia.) But it didn't take a genius to see that Kristy looked miserable. Claudia didn't seem too happy, either. She wolfed down an entire bag of potato chips before the meeting was over. That's a sure sign that she's stressed out about something.

Besides unusual quiet from Kristy and extra munching from Claudia, the meeting was pretty much business as usual. "How's your friend in ballet school doing?" Dawn asked me toward the end of the meeting.

"She keeps getting thinner, and she hasn't been feeling too good, either," I replied.

"That's such a shame," said Mary Anne.

"Quint wrote and told me it's a pretty common problem in his school," I told them. Which reminded me of his scholarship idea. I asked my friends what they thought of it.

"It's terrific!" cried Stacey.

"Do you think the school could do it?" I asked. "They already have a few scholarships for the older students. You have to audition for them, though, which means you already have to have had some training somewhere else. These kids would be beginners." I sighed deeply. "For all I know, the school might not even have the money for more scholarships."

"A corporation could sponsor the scholarship," Kristy said quietly. (Even in the height of depression, she can't stop those great ideas from coming!)

"How does that work?" Mallory asked.

"A company decides to donate money to do something worthwhile for the community," Kristy explained.

"That's awfully nice," I commented.

"I could talk to Watson and my mom about it if you like," Kristy offered. "They know all about that corporate stuff."

"Would you?" I cried happily. "That would be great."

"Sure. I'll call and let you know what they say."

I left the meeting feeling very up about the possibility of getting a scholarship or two for the kids in my class. Then I remembered Mary. I still wasn't sure what I was going to do about her. I guess I hoped she would simply stop losing weight and let me off the hook.

During class on Friday I could see that wasn't about to happen. In the dressing room it was painfully clear to me that Mary was now the thinnest in a class of thin girls. Even Mindy Howard was heavier than Mary.

It would have been one thing if Mary was just extremely thin. If that were so, I might have let it alone. (Maybe.) But Mary was falling apart. She looked awful and she seemed weak.

She *was* weak. She'd already left class early two times. As she dressed for class I saw that she was moving slowly, too slowly. It would be easy to talk with her. All I had to do was wait for everyone else to rush off to class. Mary was going to be the last one in the dressing room, so I simply waited until the others were gone.

"Can I talk to you?" I asked her, steeling myself for an unpleasant conversation.

"Jessi, don't start with me," she said irritably as she leaned over to put on her shoes.

"All I have to say is this," I began. "Either

115

you talk to Mme Noelle today about your dieting, or I will."

She looked up at me sharply. "Just exactly what would you say to her?"

"That you're dieting to the point where you're going to make yourself very sick."

"She'll laugh in your face."

"I don't think so."

"You have no right to do this, and you'd better not," Mary snapped as she turned and left the dressing room.

I had to sit down on the bench. Now *I* was the one who felt dizzy and sick to my stomach. It had taken all my courage to say what I had said to Mary. I prayed she would take me seriously because, if she didn't talk to Mme Noelle, I would have to follow through on my promise to tell Madame myself. (Was it a promise or a threat? I liked promise better.)

In a moment the wooziness passed and I hurried to class.

If I had any last doubts about what had to be done, this class put them out of my head. During center work, Mary stumbled forward during an *arabesque penché*. I was watching her. It was as if her supporting leg just gave out from under her. Naturally, the class crowded around in concern. Mary got right up, though, and went on with her dancing.

Toward the end of class, Madame gave us a fairly basic chain of steps to work on. "Now, class, starting in fifth," she commanded. *"Jeté, changement, jeté, changement, plié, tour, jeté, changement, échappé,* and *tour en l'air."* On the second *jeté* (which is a jump from one leg to the other) Mary crumbled to the ground a second time.

Once again, the class surrounded her. This time, Mary sat with her arm draped over her knee, her head hanging. She didn't try to stand or even look at anyone.

Mme Noelle came to her side and extended her hand to help Mary up. Madame is so commanding that there is no way to ignore her. Mary took her hand and got to her feet. "I'd like to speak to you after class, Madame," Mary said in a small voice.

My heart leapt with happiness and relief. Thank goodness! Something would finally be done about Mary's problem — and Mary had done it herself.

"Certainly," Mme Noelle answered. "Sit over zere and rest your ankle for now."

When class ended, I dawdled out in the hall while Mary stayed inside talking to Madame.

I wanted to be around in case she needed to talk. I didn't have to dawdle long. Inside of two minutes, Mary came hurrying out of the room, her head down. She walked right past me without ever looking up.

Now I was confused. She couldn't possibly have talked to Madame in that amount of time. I had to know what had happened.

"Mme Noelle," I said, returning to the classroom, "I need to speak to you about Mary."

"Yes?"

"I'm so worried about her. Did she tell you about her problem?"

Mme Noelle shook her head. "She began to and zen she ran from zhe room. What do you zink her problem is?"

"It's her diet. She's taken it too far and it's ruining her health. You saw what happened today."

There. I'd said it.

"Yes, I did see," Mme Noelle replied. "I will tell you somesing, *Mademoiselle* Romsey, I have seen zis before. Many times. It is tricky because it sneaks up so gradually. I suspected zis about Mary but I was not sure. Zat is why I suggested to her fazzer zat she go to a doctor."

"I don't think she did," I said.

"Nor do I." Mme Noelle began walking to-

118

ward the door. "I believe you and I should talk to Mary together. Come."

I followed Mme Noelle to the dressing room. But Mary wasn't there. The girls said she had never come in. Next we checked the ladies' room. Soft sobs were coming from the last stall.

I went to the door and knocked. "Mary," I said.

The door opened and Mary stepped out. Her eyes were puffy. She gasped when she saw Mme Noelle. "You did it!" she whispered to me.

"I did," I said. "But Madame had almost figured it out."

Mary's shoulders sagged and she seemed to realize that she had no choice but to talk about this.

Mme Noelle approached us. "Mary, dear," she said kindly. "Why is zis diet so important?"

A tear rolled down Mary's cheek. She pounded her thighs with balled-up fists. "I can't lose enough weight," she whispered through her tears. "I try and I try, but it's not enough. I'll never get to be a ballerina and it's the only thing that matters to me."

I put my hand on her shoulder. It was so sad to see her like this.

"Ozzer zings must matter to you, *made-*

119

moiselle," said Madame. "A great ballerina is more zan mere technique. A ballerina must bring passion to her dancing. To know passion you must care about ozzer people and you must love yourself, too."

Mary wiped her eyes. "But I love ballet! What if I get too fat to dance?"

"What if you get too zin to dance?" Madame countered.

Mary started to sob. I guess she was finally ready to admit to herself that she had a problem. Madame put her arm around Mary. "Come," she said. "You will dance again after you sort zis out. For now you need to rest and to talk wiss someone who can help you understand better how you are feeling. Who is coming to pick you up today?"

"My mother," Mary told her.

"Zen we will talk more when she comes," Madame told Mary.

I pulled some toilet paper from the roll and handed it to Mary.

"Yes, dry your eyes," said Madame. "Zis is not such a disaster as it seems right now. Zis is somesing zat will make life better. Life is full of many such times, you will learn zat."

Madame kept her arm around Mary and guided her out of the bathroom. I walked out behind them. "Sank you for your help, *Mademoiselle* Romsey," Mme Noelle said to me as she walked back toward the classroom with Mary.

I guess she wanted to talk with Mary some more. Or perhaps she wanted to spare Mary the embarrassment of being seen by the other girls when she was all teary-eyed and upset.

I was glad it was over, yet sad for Mary. She had worked so hard. I hoped she would be able to dance again soon.

CHAPTER 14

It seems to me that most problems that are difficult take a long time to solve. (Deciding what to do about Mary was one of those things.) And others are solved with a snap of the fingers.

For instance, the scholarship seemed like an impossible project — but it turned out to be a breeze.

When I arrived at the Brewers to baby-sit on Saturday, Kristy was grinning from ear to ear. "Watson is at his office right now," she told me as she got ready to leave. "He's talking to his accountant about the scholarship! He and Mom were going to go to this luncheon but he cancelled and Mom went by herself."

"I'm confused!" I said.

"I guess you would be. Okay, here's the deal. When I asked Watson about corporations, he got all excited and said we didn't have to bother with a corporation."

"Why not?" I asked, still confused.

"Because he's thinking about offering the scholarship himself!"

"You're kidding!" I cried.

"It's not definite," Kristy said quickly. "I shouldn't even have told you. So don't be too disappointed if it falls through."

"Why would it fall through?" I asked.

"He has to talk to his accountant first," Kristy explained. "Watson never makes a move without him."

"I hope his accountant likes ballet."

"I don't think that matters," Kristy said as she grabbed her jacket. "It just has to do with money." She pulled up the zipper. "Well, I'm off. Karen and Andrew are over at the Papadakises', so it's just you and Emily for now. Unless Shannon stops over. She does seem to do that a lot lately."

At the mention of Shannon, a tense, unhappy look swept over Kristy. I decided this might be a good time to speak up. "Kristy, are you . . . uh . . . okay?" I asked.

"Sure," Kristy said, looking down.

"You know, we all like Shannon, but we really love you, too. I mean, Shannon is fun, but you're — you're Kristy."

Kristy laughed. "I'm Kristy, all right." She looked up at me. "Thanks, Jessi. I know what you're trying to say and . . . just thanks."

"You're welcome."

Kristy left for her meeting and I was left to play with Emily. I had been warned by Stacey about Emily's "puway" game so I watched her like a hawk and managed to keep track of everyone's possessions. Mostly we sat in the family room and played Emily Michelle's version of Shark Attack.

Kristy's mom came home first. "How was your luncheon?" I asked, putting away the game pieces.

"Oh, you know how those things are," she said. (I had no idea how they were.) "The same old warmed-over chicken and boring speeches, but it was for the Children's Hospital so I suppose it was worth it."

Just then I heard the front door close. A moment later Watson walked in. "Hi, honey," Mrs. Brewer greeted him. "What did Stewart have to say?"

"He says we can do it right away!" Watson looked at me and a beaming smile crossed his face. "I can offer your school two full scholarships," he told me happily. "The money is available as soon as you need it and it will be there every year."

My jaw dropped, but no sound came out.

124

This was so amazing! So awesomely wonderful!

"Thank you so much!" I finally said when I found my voice. "Thank you so, so, sooooo much."

"You are very welcome," Watson replied. He pulled his wallet from the inside pocket of his jacket and, for a moment, I thought he was going to hand me the money there and then. But instead he gave me his business card. "Have someone from the school call me. That's my office number, and you know the home number, of course."

I wanted to hug Watson, but I didn't feel that I really knew him well enough for that. Instead, I just stood there grinning like crazy.

"Well, I have some work to do in my study, so if you'll excuse me," said Watson. He left the room with a bounce in his step. From down the hall I heard him begin to whistle "The Dance of the Sugarplum Fairies," from *The Nutcracker Suite*.

"He seems very pleased," Mrs. Brewer said happily.

"He's not the only one," I told her.

"We're glad to help, Jessi. And thanks for taking care of Emily."

Mrs. Brewer drove me home. I couldn't stop

thinking about the scholarships. What kids would get them? Who would decide? What would Mme Noelle say when I gave her the news? It was all so exciting!

I hadn't been home a half hour when Kristy called. "You've really made Watson happy," she told me. "He's been whistling ballet tunes since I came back."

"This is so wonderful of him and your mom," I said.

"Hey, what's the fun of having money if you can't spread it around a little?"

"It wouldn't have happened if you hadn't brought it up to them. Thanks a million, Kristy."

"All I did was ask. See you Monday."

On Monday, Kristy seemed much more like her old self. (Nothing cheers Kristy up like accomplishing something.)

On Tuesday I reached my dance class early. I was bursting to tell Mme Noelle that Watson was willing to donate two scholarships. When I did, Madame smiled and clapped her hands together. "You are a mind reader!" she cried. "I had ze same idea and I have been contacting company after company looking for a corporate sponsorship. I had given up totally."

"Well, now you have it," I said.

"Come, let us tell Mme Dupre the happy

news." We went down to the practice room and met up with Mme Dupre as she was going in the door.

Her hands flew to her cheeks when we told her. "This is too amazing!" she said. "Oh, this makes me so happy."

"Me, too," I agreed.

I gave Watson's business card to Mme Noelle and she hurried off to call him. When Mme Dupre and I went into class I looked around for Mary. I wasn't too surprised that she wasn't there.

At the sight of Mme Dupre, the class quieted down. "I have a wonderful announcement," she told the kids. "We have scholarships available for two students. The assistants and I will choose the students based on our evaluation. The ones we feel have the most potential will be given the scholarships. It will be a difficult choice, I assure you. If you wish to be considered to study further, please write your name on a list as you leave today. I will send a notice home to your parents, as well. You will have until next week to put your name on the list."

A murmur of excitement spread through the class. I wondered which kids would sign up.

"And now, today after warm-up we will begin work on a recital," Mme Dupre continued. "We will be putting on a dance program at the end of our classes. I have worked out an original dance for you. Let's begin. We have much to do in a short time."

Mme Dupre had come up with a really great program to teach the kids. It would be easy for them to learn since it was a combination of the steps they'd been taught and even some of the warm-up exercises. Madame called it, "Morning in the City." Mr. Tsuji played lively musical pieces by an America composer named George Gershwin. Gershwin had composed the music for an old movie called *An American in Paris*. His music is really uplifting.

The dance began with the class sitting in their separate groups, bent over touching their toes. Then group by group, they "awakened" each doing a different stretching exercise.

The groups continued to dance together as units. One group *jeté*d into an imaginary subway and then did small *échappé* jumps as they held their hands up like subway riders holding the straps. Another group performed *arabesques* as they pretended to greet one another on the street.

Madame singled out Devon to execute a series of *pas de chat* jumps as he pretended to cross a busy street. Martha was selected to dance a short solo. At a certain beat, everyone was to freeze in place while she performed a *bourée*, followed by a *pas de chat*, and end with a single *pirouette*, which is a spin on one leg. (Martha was the only student in class who was ready for it.)

"Will we have costumes?" asked Yvonne, who was featured as a crossing guard.

"Next week I want you to bring in hats, as many different kinds of hats as you can find," she told the kids.

The class was over all too soon. While the other volunteers and I finished up, I saw Mme Dupre talk to the parents who had gathered at the door. I assumed she was telling them about the recital and the scholarships.

At the end of class, Martha ran to her mother. Her eyes were bright and excited as she spoke to her. Once again, I noticed that her mother was looking at me.

Since I was into speaking up these days, I decided to introduce myself. "Hi," I said. "I'm Jessi. I just wanted to find out if Martha will be applying for the scholarship."

"Do you think she should?" the woman asked, speaking with that great accent that comes from the Caribbean islands.

"I definitely do!"

Martha's mother pressed her lips together thoughtfully. "I know Martha is talented," she said after a moment. "I worked very hard for the extra money to enroll her in ballet classes."

"She seems to have remembered everything she learned," I commented. "Why did you stop?"

"A neighbor told me I was wasting my money. She said there is no room for people of color in the ballet. I don't want Martha to set her heart on a dream which cannot be."

"Is that why you've been watching me?" I guessed.

The woman seemed embarrassed. "Forgive me if I have been rude. You are the only black student I have seen in this school. I was wondering how you feel about your future."

"I feel good about it," I told her. "Classical ballet is changing. It's changed a lot already. And some companies, like the Alvin Ailey dancers, are mostly non-white. Judith Jamison is a very respected dancer from that company, even though she's not a classical ballerina. I just think there's a lot of opportunity. I can't let other people stop me from doing what I want, and I don't think they'll be able to. I've already danced in several professional productions."

"You have?" she asked.

"I was one of the swan maidens in *Swan Lake*," I told her proudly. "And I've danced in other productions."

"I'm glad we talked," the woman said. "Martha loves this class. She speaks of you all the time."

"She's very special," I told her mother. "And she's really talented."

At that, I saw Martha's beautiful smile once again. It warmed me as much as any room full of applause.

CHAPTER 15

Our Wednesday BSC meeting was almost as busy as the one on Monday. And because we were getting booked up fast, I knew we were going to have to call on our associate members — Logan and Shannon.

By now all of us were aware that Shannon had become a touchy subject. So a big silence followed Mary Anne's announcement that no one was free to sit for Charlotte Johanssen on Friday. Not even Logan.

"We'll have to call Shannon," said Claudia, breaking the deadly quiet. "Want me to call her, Kristy?"

"No, I'll call." Kristy took the phone and punched in Shannon's number. "Hi, it's me, Kristy," she said into the phone. "Listen, I want to apologize for the other day. I was wrong and I had no reason to talk to you like that. I just felt left out and sort of jealous, I guess."

I had to give Kristy credit. That took guts — especially saying it in front of a room full of people.

Shannon must have told her it was all right, because Kristy went on to ask her about the baby-sitting job. She was free to take it and Kristy hung up, looking relieved.

"We still have a problem," Claudia said. "We'd still like to keep seeing Shannon, Kristy, but we don't want to hurt your feelings."

"I like Shannon, too," Kristy told us. "I wish I could hang out with her, but I don't seem able to with my schedule. When you all spent so much time with her I began to feel she was replacing me. I didn't like it."

"Replacing you?" Dawn cried with a laugh. "I don't think anyone could!"

There was a general murmur of agreement, which I'm sure made Kristy feel good.

"I have an idea," said Mary Anne. "Why don't we ask Shannon to attend our regular meetings every now and then? She has the time now. And she could drive over and back with you, Kristy. That way the two of you could have some time together."

"Hey, great!" Kristy agreed. "I should have thought of that."

"You're not the only one who has great

ideas!" Mary Anne said, pretending to be insulted.

"Speaking of great ideas, I heard about the scholarships," said Stacey. "Way to go, Watson!"

"Would any of you guys like to come to the recital? It's not this Saturday, but next Saturday at the school," I said.

"I'll be there with my parents," Kristy told me. "I wouldn't miss the awarding of the first Watson and Elizabeth Brewer Dance Scholarships."

"That's what they're calling them?" I asked.

"Mme Noelle insisted," Kristy said.

All the BSC members wanted to come to the recital, which made me really happy. "Should we call Shannon and invite her?" Mallory asked.

"Absolutely," said Kristy.

By the last class before the recital, the kids knew their parts pretty well. At the end of class, Mme Dupre gave us volunteers a list of the kids who had applied for the scholarships — a little less than half the class. (I wasn't surprised to see that Nora and Jane weren't on the list, but I was a little surprised that plump, bouncy Yvonne hadn't applied.) "Pick the two children you think shows the most promise and write their names on a piece of paper," Mme Dupre instructed us.

We passed the list around and then made our selections. Everyone picked pretty fast. I guess we'd made up our minds in advance.

After a busy rehearsal, Darcy suggested a trip to Burger King. We bundled up and headed down the block. "Where's Mary been?" Sue asked once we were settled in with our food.

"She hasn't been feeling well. I guess she needed to take some time off," I said, not wanting to gossip. Actually, Mme Noelle had told me Mary was being treated by two different doctors — a medical doctor and a psychiatrist. Plus, her family went to the counseling, too.

"I saw Mary in school," said Vince, breaking into my thoughts. "It looked to me like she put on a few pounds."

"Good, maybe she's feeling better," I said, sipping my soda. It was the best news I'd heard all day.

"This show is going to be cool," Raul said as he put down his burger.

"Now that the class is over, what do you think of Mme Dupre?" I asked him.

"I think I misjudged her," Raul admitted. "She's pretty cool."

"Yeah, there was a method to her madness, after all," added Darcy. "Remember how undisciplined the kids were when they first came in? Look at them now!"

"It's a big difference," I agreed.

"Huge," said Sue. "I feel good about it, like we really helped her accomplish something."

On the afternoon of the recital I was all over the place, helping kids pin on hats and apply makeup. We were in the school's small auditorium. The only scenery was a cityscape backdrop borrowed from another production.

The kids were nervous and excited as the audience filled with their family members. I peeked out from a stage wing and saw my friends filing into a row near the front. (Kristy and Shannon sat next to one another.)

Following them were Watson and Kristy's mom. A few minutes later I saw my parents come in with Aunt Cecelia, Becca, and Squirt. Mama talked with Mme Noelle as they walked down the aisle. An awful lot of people had turned out for our informal little show.

Soon, the big moment came when Mr. Tsuji played the opening music. The kids ran onto the stage and took their places on the floor.

I'd like to say the production was flawless. But I'd be lying. Some kids stood when they were supposed to kneel. Others turned right when the rest of the group was turning left. But, on the whole, it was a very good show.

I was really proud of the students. (They looked *so* cute in their hats — baseball caps, flowered hats, a train engineer's hat, a nurse's cap, cowboy hats, you name it!)

The audience must have liked the show, too. They jumped to their feet and applauded like crazy when it was over. The kids took their bows and each one of them was beaming from ear to ear.

Mme Dupre walked out on stage and both the kids and the audience clapped for her. She told us volunteers and Mr. Tsuji to take a bow. The applause continued and it felt really good.

When the clapping had stopped, Mme Noelle came onto the stage. "I will now announce ze winners of ze Watson and Elizabeth Brewer Dance Scholarships," she told the audience as the kids took seats on the stage. While we waited in suspense, she asked Watson and Kristy's mom to stand. She thanked them for their generosity. They smiled and Watson said he was glad to be able to do it.

Mme Noelle then turned to the class of children. "I am sorry zere can be only two winners. You are all so talented. And you are all winners in my eyes. I invite you to return in ze spring when we will offer zis class again. We will be proud to have you."

Finally Mme Noelle took a slip of paper from

her pocket. "Ze winners of the scholarships are Martha Roberts and Devon Ramirez," she said.

My cheeks hurt from smiling so hard. Devon and Martha got to their feet. Martha was so happy, she forgot to be shy. She smiled and hugged herself in disbelief.

Even more surprising, Devon was so thrilled, he forgot to be cool! "Yes!" he cried, leaping into the air right there on stage.

Mme Dupre guided them over to Mme Noelle who shook their hands. "I know you will both work hard and be worthy of our faith in you," she told them both.

When the program at last was over, Martha ran to me. She wrapped her arms around me and squeezed tight. In the wings I saw her mother. She was dressed in a gray suit. In her hands was a corsage box and I could see tears of pride brimming in her eyes.

On another part of the stage Devon was busily "slapping five" with anyone he could find. Then he ran off to greet his father.

"Well, it's all over for now," said Darcy, draping her arm across my shoulder. "Maybe we can still go out for burgers on Tuesdays, though."

"That would be terrific," I said.

I found my friends in the audience. "That

sure was a success," Kristy told me. "I really liked it."

"So did I," Shannon agreed.

"All right, Jessi!" Mal cheered.

"Is Mary here?" Dawn asked quietly.

I looked around the audience but didn't see any sign of her. "No. I wish she had come," I said. "She did a lot to help these kids. I'm sure she would have been proud."

"I took some pictures," said Claudia, holding up her camera. "I could make copies for you to send her."

"She'd like that," I said, and smiled.

Sometimes I wonder why I work so hard at my dance; why I let it be so important to me and take up so much of my life.

Today was one of those days when I didn't have to wonder, though. Today was the kind of day when I couldn't imagine anything more worthwhile!

About the Author

ANN M. MARTIN did *a lot* of baby-sitting when she was growing up in Princeton, New Jersey. She is a former editor of books for children, and was graduated from Smith College.

Ms. Martin lives in New York City with her cats, Mouse and Rosie. She likes ice cream and *I Love Lucy;* and she hates to cook.

Ann Martin's Apple Paperbacks include *Yours Turly, Shirley; Ten Kids, No Pets; With You and Without You; Bummer Summer;* and all the other books in the Baby-sitters Club series.

Look for #62

KRISTY AND THE WORST KID EVER

It seemed as if we had all barely gotten settled back down in the kitchen when a horrible new noise met our ears.

Crash!

Somehow I wasn't surprised to find Shannon backing in circles in the living room, pawning at her face, which had a scarf tied over it so she couldn't see. She backed into a bookcase and knocked half a dozen books off, then yelped when one hit her.

"What's going on?" I demanded. Talk about *déjà vu*!

Hannie explained, "It's a game. We were seeing if Shannon could find her bone blindfolded. We hid it on the chair."

"Who did this?" I asked, reaching down to untie the scarf. Shannon, none the worse for the wear, gave the air a couple of experimental sniffs, then zeroed in on her bone.

Everyone looked at Lou. What a surprise.

Lou shrugged. "I used to know a dog who could do that."

I took a deep breath. "Even if you did, Shannon is just a puppy and she doesn't understand."

"She's not very smart," said Lou.

David Michael came in just in time to hear her words. (I'd wonderd where he was. I didn't *think* he'd let Lou do that to Shannon.)

"She is too!" said David Michael. "Especially for a puppy."

"I wouldn't have a dumb old dog as dumb as her," said Lou.

"That enough," I said. With the help of the rest of the BSC we got everyone settled down and involved in quieter pursuits (we hoped), then made our weary way back to the breakfast table.

"Silence is golden," sighed Mary Anne as we finished breakfast at last.

"Yeah," I agreed. I looked around at everyone. "And you know what? I feel sorry for Lou. But she *is* the absolute worst kid I have ever met."

Not one single person disagreed with me.

**Read all the latest books
in the Baby-sitters Club series
by Ann M. Martin**

144

8 *The Baby-sitters at Shadow Lake*
Campfires, cute guys, *and* a mystery — the baby-sitters are in for a week of summer fun!

Mysteries:

5 *Mary Anne and the Secret in the Attic*
Mary Anne discovers a secret about her past and now she's afraid of the future!

6 *The Mystery at Claudia's House*
Claudia's room has been ransacked! Can the Baby-sitters track down whodunnit?

7 *Dawn and the Disappearing Dogs*
Someone's been stealing dogs all over Stoneybrook!

8 *Jessi and the Jewel Thieves*
Jessi and her friend Quint are busy tailing two jewel thieves all over the Big Apple!

Special Edition (Readers' Request):
Logan's Story
Being a boy baby-sitter isn't easy!

by Ann M. Martin

More titles...

The Baby-sitters Club titles continued...

- ❑ MG43568-X #39 Poor Mallory! — $3.25
- ❑ MG44082-9 #40 Claudia and the Middle School Mystery — $3.25
- ❑ MG43570-1 #41 Mary Anne Versus Logan — $3.25
- ❑ MG44083-7 #42 Jessi and the Dance School Phantom — $3.25
- ❑ MG43572-8 #43 Stacey's Emergency — $3.25
- ❑ MG43573-6 #44 Dawn and the Big Sleepover — $3.25
- ❑ MG43574-4 #45 Kristy and the Baby Parade — $3.25
- ❑ MG43569-8 #46 Mary Anne Misses Logan — $3.25
- ❑ MG44971-0 #47 Mallory on Strike — $3.25
- ❑ MG43571-X #48 Jessi's Wish — $3.25
- ❑ MG44970-2 #49 Claudia and the Genius of Elm Street — $3.25
- ❑ MG44969-9 #50 Dawn's Big Date — $3.25
- ❑ MG44968-0 #51 Stacey's Ex-Best Friend — $3.25
- ❑ MG44966-4 #52 Mary Anne + 2 Many Babies — $3.25
- ❑ MG44967-2 #53 Kristy for President — $3.25
- ❑ MG44965-6 #54 Mallory and the Dream Horse — $3.25
- ❑ MG44964-8 #55 Jessi's Gold Medal — $3.25
- ❑ MG45657-1 #56 Keep Out, Claudia! — $3.25
- ❑ MG45658-X #57 Dawn Saves the Planet — $3.25
- ❑ MG45659-8 #58 Stacey's Choice — $3.25
- ❑ MG45660-1 #59 Mallory Hates Boys (and Gym) — $3.25
- ❑ MG45662-8 #60 Mary Anne's Makeover — $3.50
- ❑ MG45663-6 #61 Jessi and the Awful Secret — $3.50
- ❑ MG45575-3 Logan's Story   Special Edition Readers' Request — $3.25

Available wherever you buy books...or use this order form.

Scholastic Inc., P.O. Box 7502, 2931 E. McCarty Street, Jefferson City, MO 65102

Please send me the books I have checked above. I am enclosing $_____
(please add $2.00 to cover shipping and handling). Send check or money order - no
cash or C.O.D.s please.

Name _____

Address _____

City_____ State/Zip_____

Tell us your birth date! _____

Please allow four to six weeks for delivery. Offer good in the U.S. only. Sorry, mail orders are not
available to residents of Canada. Prices subject to change.

It's a Super Special Month!

YOU CAN WIN A TRIP TO WALT DISNEY WORLD RESORT®!

Enter The Winter Super Special Giveaway for The Baby-sitters Club® and Baby-sitters Little Sister® fans!

Visit Walt Disney World Resort...and experience all the excitement of Peter Pan Tinkerbell, and a whole cast of characters! We'll send the **Grand Prize Winner** this Giveaway and his/her parent or guardian (age 21 or older) on an all-expens paid trip, for 5 days and 4 nights, to Walt Disney World Resort in Florida!

10 Second Prize Winners get a Baby-sitters Club Record Album!
25 Third Prize Winners get a Baby-sitters Club T-shirt!

Early Bird Bonus!

100 early entries will receive a Baby-sitters Club calendar! But hurry!
To qualify, your entry must be postmarked by December 1, 1992.

Just fill in the coupon below or write the information on a 3" x 5" piece of paper and mail
THE WINTER SUPER SPECIAL GIVEAWAY, P.O. Box 7500, Jefferson City, MO 65102
Return by March 31, 1993.

Rules: Entries must be postmarked by March 31, 1993. Winners will be picked at random and notified by mail. No purchase necessary. Valid only i
U.S. Void where prohibited. Taxes on prizes are the responsibility of the winners and their immediate families. Employees of Scholastic Inc.; its agen
affiliates, subsidiaries; and their immediate families are not eligible. For a complete list of winners, send a self-addressed stamped envelope after
March 31, 1993 to: The Winter Super Special Giveaway Winners List, at the address provided above.

- -

The Winter Super Special Giveaway

Name _____ Age _____

Street _____

City _____ State/Zip _____

Where did you buy this book?

☐ Bookstore   ☐ Drugstore   ☐ Supermarket   ☐ Library
☐ Book Club   ☐ Book Fair   ☐ Other_____ (specify)   B